W9-BMN-613

ALSO FROM JOE BOOKS

Disney Frozen: The Cinestory

Disney Princess Treasury

Disney Pixar Treasury

Cinestory Comic

JOE BOOKS INC

Published in the United States by Joe Books
Publisher: Adam Fortier
President: Jody Colero
CEO: Jay Firestone
567 Queen St W, Toronto, ON M5V 2B6
www.joebooks.com

Library and Archives Canada Cataloguing in Publication
information is available upon request.

ISBN 978-1-926516-05-9 (Joe Books edition, US)

First Joe Books Editions: March 2015

3 5 7 9 10 8 6 4 2

Copyright © 2015 Disney Enterprises, Inc. All rights reserved.

Published in the United States by Joe Books, Inc.
by arrangement with Joe Books, Inc.

No portion of this publication may be reproduced or transmitted, in any form or
by any means, without the express written permission of the copyright holders.

Names, characters, places, and incidents featured in this publication are either the product of the author's imagination or are used fictitiously. Any resemblance to actual persons (living or dead), events, institutions, or locales, without satiric intent, is coincidental.

Joe Books™ is a trademark of Joe Books, Inc. Joe Books® and
the Joe Books Logo are trademarks of Joe Books, Inc.,
registered in various categories and countries.
All rights reserved.

Printed in USA through Avenue4 Communications at Cenveo/Richmond, Virginia

For information regarding the CPSIA on this printed material, call:
(203) 595-3636 and provide reference

#RICH - 592792.

Cinestory Comic

ADAPTED BY
Robert Simpson, Erik Burnham, and Jeremy Barlow

INTRODUCTION BY
Leonard Maltin

LETTERING AND LAYOUT
Salvador Navarro, Eduardo Alpuente, Alberto Garrido

DESIGNER
Heidi Roux

SENIOR EDITOR
Carolynn Prior

SENIOR EDITOR
Robert Simpson

PRODUCTION COORDINATOR
Stephanie Alouche

BY LEONARD MALTIN

Cinderella is one of Walt Disney's best-loved films, and it isn't hard to see why. It has all the ingredients that we associate with a Disney classic. Warm, funny, empathetic characters; beautiful animation and design; catchy songs; and a foolproof story. It is a fairy tale—the genre that always brought out the best in Disney and his team, and continues to work its magic in such modern-day studio films as *Tangled* and *Frozen*.

Chris Buck, the co-director of *Frozen*, understands the power of these mythical stories. He remembers seeing *Pinocchio* as a little boy. "Monstro the Whale scared me to death," he says, "but it all came out OK. I went on this wonderful roller coaster of emotions. I think deep down it does teach children that yes, it may be scary right now, but at the end, with a little bit of hope, things can be all right." *Cinderella* puts its viewers through the emotional wringer, along with its heroine and her friends, and then provides that happy ending that makes the journey so rewarding: a catharsis, if you will.

The story of *Cinderella* dates back more than 300 years and shows no sign of losing its potency or relevance.

Walt Disney turned to this storytelling staple in his first cartoon series, the *Laugh-O-Grams*: his Cinderella was released back in 1922. When that same story went into production as a feature several decades later, it provided many challenges to its creators, who knew there was a great deal at stake. Had it failed, it might have spelled the end of Disney animation.

To explain, we must turn back the clock more than a decade before *Cinderella*'s release in 1950. When Disney decided to embark upon a feature-length animated cartoon in the mid-

1930s, many people in the movie industry thought he was headed for failure. Who would want to see a cartoon that ran more than seven minutes? Certainly no grown-ups would pay admission for a film like that. How could it ever recover its enormous cost?

Of course, *Snow White and the Seven Dwarfs* turned out to be an enormous, worldwide hit. It should have put Walt Disney's company on firm financial footing for years to come, but things didn't work out that way. For one thing, he spent freely on his next two features, *Pinocchio* (which enjoyed a fair degree of success) and *Fantasia* (which didn't). The outbreak of war in Europe robbed the company of precious income from overseas markets. Walt and his brother Roy struggled to stay in business during these turbulent years.

Their only real success in this period was *Bambi*, which had been in the works for five years. But there wasn't enough money or manpower to launch another ambitious, story-driven feature.

By the late 1940s, Walt Disney knew there was only one way to put his studio back in gear, artistically and financially: by giving moviegoers around the globe what they craved, a fairy tale in the same vein as *Snow White*. To expedite the production process, once his story team had a decent screenplay and his songwriters had crafted a handful of agreeable tunes, he shot the entire film in live-action, with actors pantomiming their roles on rudimentary sets, to give his animators a solid blueprint to follow. (They had used live-action reference for their earlier features, but not to this extent.)

For Disney and his crew, the question was how to breathe new life into such a time-worn tale, originated by Charles Perrault in the 17th century. Every child knows the story of Cinderella, who is abused by her cruel stepmother and stepsisters. Her fairy godmother transforms her into a ravishing beauty so she can attend a royal ball, where she completely captivates the Prince. At the stroke of midnight, she must flee or be revealed as a scullery maid. Running off, she drops one glass slipper. The Prince is determined to find the girl he loves, and tests the slipper on each maiden in the kingdom, until he is reunited with Cinderella...and they live happily ever after.

Walt was determined not to make a mere replica of *Snow White and the Seven Dwarfs*.

Task number one: make sure Cinderella is likable, so we root for her right from the start. He assigned two of his best artists, Marc Davis and Eric Larson, to share the job of animating the lovely heroine. Like Snow White, she has a special relationship with the birds and animals around her, which immediately endears her to us. She is, as the narrator tells us, ever gentle and kind. But unlike Snow White, Cinderella is more fully formed. Despite the fact that she is browbeaten on a daily basis, she refuses to succumb to despair. She makes the best of things and strives to remain positive in spite of all the abuse heaped upon her on a daily basis.

That's one reason Disney's *Cinderella* still resonates with girls and young women today. Jennifer Lee, the screenwriter and co-director of *Frozen*, cites this as her favorite Disney classic. She says, "What *Cinderella* meant to me—I had a tough childhood—was, 'Anything is possible. This may change. Things don't stay the same' and I will always hold that dear."

In spite of the comedy-relief characters that surround her and provide much of the entertainment (and most of the laughs) in this film, animator Marc Davis reminded latter-day interviewers that "Cinderella carries the story. If you don't believe in her, it doesn't matter how good or funny or interesting the rest of the characters are—the picture just doesn't work. With Cinderella, you could see the hurt and see the feeling."

It's the way the animal characters interact with Cinderella, and parallel her story (sometimes as observers, sometimes as participants) that makes them so integral to the picture. The idea of interweaving their actions is introduced right at the start of the film: a flock of friendly bluebirds awaken Cinderella and help her get up and dressed as they sing together. In the midst of this cheery scene, we meet Jaq the mouse, who is roused out of his sleep by the music. He stretches a yawn, licks his hair, brushes it back (though it instantly falls back into disarray) and finds, to his annoyance, that his tail has become knotted during the night.

Soon afterwards, he beckons Cinderella downstairs, where she rescues a chubby little mouse who's been caught in a trap overnight. She not only saves his life but welcomes him into the household, naming him Octavius—or Gus, for short.

Aside from the mice and bluebirds, the household menagerie includes a sleepy dog named Bruno and a horse who's stabled just outside the castle where Cinderella lives with her cruel stepmother, Lady Tremaine, and her ill-tempered daughters Anastasia and Drizella. The key non-human antagonist in this rendering of the story is a wily cat named Lucifer who annoys our heroine and terrorizes her little friends.

Throughout the film, the actions of the humans and the animals are perfectly integrated, with one scene seamlessly leading into another. One can imagine the endless work by story people in the animation department to achieve this perfectly rounded result.

Comedy is also derived from the characters of the King and his Grand Duke. The King is upset because his son is single, and apparently has no interest in women. How will his majesty ever experience the joy of having grandchildren if things keep up as they are? He and the Grand Duke decide to hold a ball, inviting every eligible female in the kingdom, in the hope that the Prince will find one to his liking. These two figures, who serve an important story function as well as adding humor to the screenplay, would inspire similar characters in Disney's next major fairy tale, *Sleeping Beauty*.

Ward Kimball won the assignment of animating Bruno and joked that he was one of the few principal artists who didn't have to consult live-action footage in his work. He still hadn't figured out Bruno's attitude or personality when Walt happened to visit Kimball's home one day—they were both railroad buffs—and noticed Kimball's cat Fiji curling around his leg. Disney told his animator, "There's the model for your cat!" It's no coincidence that a short time later, Kimball was chosen to animate the Cheshire Cat in *Alice in Wonderland*: the two characters share a devilish grin that's apparent in the still-frames in this book.

What you can't appreciate in a printed version of Disney's *Cinderella* is the high-pitched voices that emanate from the household birds and those two heroic mice. When the tiny creatures sing out as they take on the task of creating a ball gown for Cinderella, in a ditty officially called "The Work Song," it's irresistible.

Incidentally, the voices of Jaq and Gus—sped up in the recording process—were performed by James "Jimmy" MacDonald, a beloved figure at the Disney studio who created and invented innumerable sound effects during his forty-year career. The Scottish-born musician and jack-of-all-trades also inherited the job of voicing Mickey Mouse from Walt Disney when the boss decided to retire himself as Mickey's alter ego in the 1940s.

There were no "celebrity" voices on the soundtrack of Cinderella, but the characters are all perfectly cast. Band vocalist Ilene Woods is just right as the speaking and singing voice of our heroine. Experienced radio actress Eleanor Audley is memorably menacing as Lady Tremaine. Tremaine would go on to give life to one of Disney's most memorable villains, Maleficent, in 1959's *Sleeping Beauty*.) Longtime animation voice artist Lucille Bliss (soon to be cast as Crusader Rabbit in the early TV cartoon series) is hilariously expressive as Anastasia. And future TV talk-show host Mike Douglas, then a band singer, is just right as Prince Charming. Ironically, the gentle voice who narrates the introductory scenes belongs to another versatile radio actress, Betty Lou Gerson, who made her mark in Disney history a decade later as Cruella de Vil in *101 Dalmatians.*

Songs were an integral part of every Disney feature. For *Cinderella,* Walt sought out the pop songwriters who had a novelty hit in 1947 with a song popularized by Perry Como called "Chi-Baba, Chi-Baba (My Bambino Go to Sleep)." As unlikely as that might sound, Disney's instincts were—as usual—correct. Mack David, Jerry Livingston, and Al Hoffman understood the nature of writing on assignment. They turned out a number of songs for this feature that not only suited the characters and situations but enjoyed great popularity on radio and the record charts.

The first song we hear, as Cinderella wakes up, is "A Dream is a Wish Your Heart Makes," as lovely a ballad as ever graced a Disney score. More important, it expresses our heroine's positive outlook as well as her wistful yearning for a better life.

Every song serves a specific purpose. The staging of "Sing Sweet Nightingale" is particularly ingenious. It was apparently Walt's idea to have Cinderella reflected in a series of soap bubbles as she scrubs the floor, with each bubble representing another voice in a chorus of Cinderellas. The technique of overdubbing was still relatively new at this time and must have made a strong impression on audiences in 1950.

The *pièce de resistance* is "Bibbidi-Bobbidi Boo," a kissin' cousin to "Chi-Baba, Chi-Baba" that wound up earning an Academy Award nomination as Best Song. It is memorably introduced by Cinderella's fairy godmother, voiced by veteran radio actress Verna Felton, and forms the centerpiece of the film's most memorable sequence. (On radio, and later television, Felton often played battle-axe characters; she made her Disney debut as one of the snooty elephants who pokes cruel fun at Dumbo in the movie of the same name. Yet she brings just the right touch of motherly affection to this all-important character in *Cinderella*.)

There is real magic in this scene, even though we know what's coming. The Disney story men knew how to take their time playing out the particulars, and enjoyed making the fairy godmother slightly absent-minded. First, she forgets where she put her magic wand, then she neglects to transform Cinderella's tattered dress into an exquisite ball gown until the very last minute. Our heroine's heartfelt thank-you endears her to us all the more.

The character design in Cinderella runs the gamut, from the surprisingly realistic rendering of the cruel stepmother to the broadly cartoonish look of Jaq, Gus, and Lucifer. What may be less obvious is the stylization of the settings, part of a transition that the Disney studio was undergoing in its approach to animation at this time. Look at the trees, the landscape, the castles: they no longer represent a literal approach, inspired by European storybook illustration. These designs are more fanciful and modern.

The staging and use of color were the work of four talented artists: Mary Blair, Claude Coats, John Hench, and Don DaGradi. All made valuable contributions to Disney films over the years, but Blair's work has become a touchstone for many contemporary artists, including the leading lights at Pixar. She not only favored unusual combinations of colors but made striking use of them for dramatic purposes: observe the backgrounds in the wrenching scene where the stepsisters willfully tear Cinderella's ball gown to shreds, in a series of artfully edited closeups. By the end of this terrible encounter the backdrop is a deep red, reflecting the heightened emotions stirred onscreen (and in us).

That scene is a tour-de-force, but it's indicative of how canny the Disney team had become in staging sequences to insure the greatest response from an audience. There are many other examples in *Cinderella*, many involving the heartless scheming of Lady Tremaine (right up until the final moments) but most notably when the little mice realize they must somehow rescue their friend Cinderella from her room upstairs, by stealing the key from the stepmother's pocket and making their way up a daunting flight of steps—seen from their point of view.

Film critic Roger Ebert revisited the film on its theatrical reissue and made special note of this scene, writing, "When those little mice bust a gut trying to drag that key up hundreds of stairs in order to free Cinderella, I don't care how many Kubrick pictures, you've seen, it's still exciting."

Just as Stanley Kubrick put his personal stamp on every movie he made, Walt Disney was the driving force behind *Cinderella*. Looking back in 1981, animator Wolfgang Reitherman said, "There was nothing that escaped Walt, not even the smallest detail. He reviewed everything from the story sketches and character development sketches to all the idea sketches and animation drawings. And for Cinderella we made somewhere near a million drawings. Walt saw every single one.

"He had a habit of roaming and would turn up at the most unlikely spots when you'd least expect him. We'd call him for a story meeting to show him the new storyboards, and inevitably he'd already seen the boards sometime during the middle of the night before and would throw out some new ideas."

Animator Marc Davis once remarked, "Somebody asked

Walt what his favorite scene was in all the animation that we had done and he said, 'Well, I guess it would have to be where Cinderella got her gown.' I think he particularly liked this scene because here the poor comes out on top. In a sense Walt was a Cinderella—he had very humble beginnings. He believed that good would triumph over evil and that was true in all the films that he had anything to do with."

That, more than anything else, is what keeps *Cinderella* so fresh and vital: the story is heartfelt. It was often observed that Walt Disney didn't have to rely on previews or research to know how people would react to a film, because he responded just the way his audience did. This film is living proof of that.

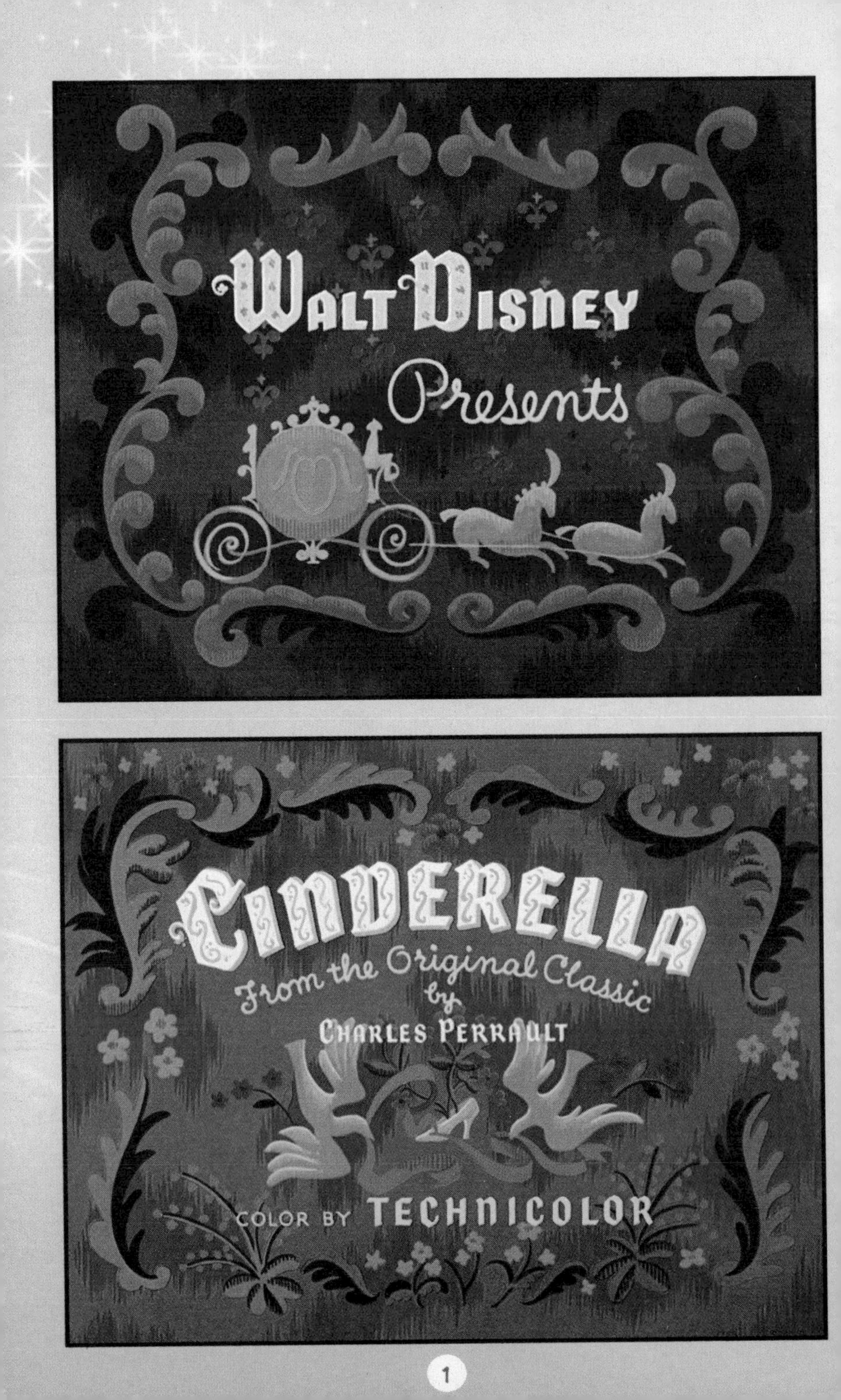
Walt Disney
Presents
Cinderella
From the Original Classic
by
Charles Perrault
COLOR BY TECHNICOLOR

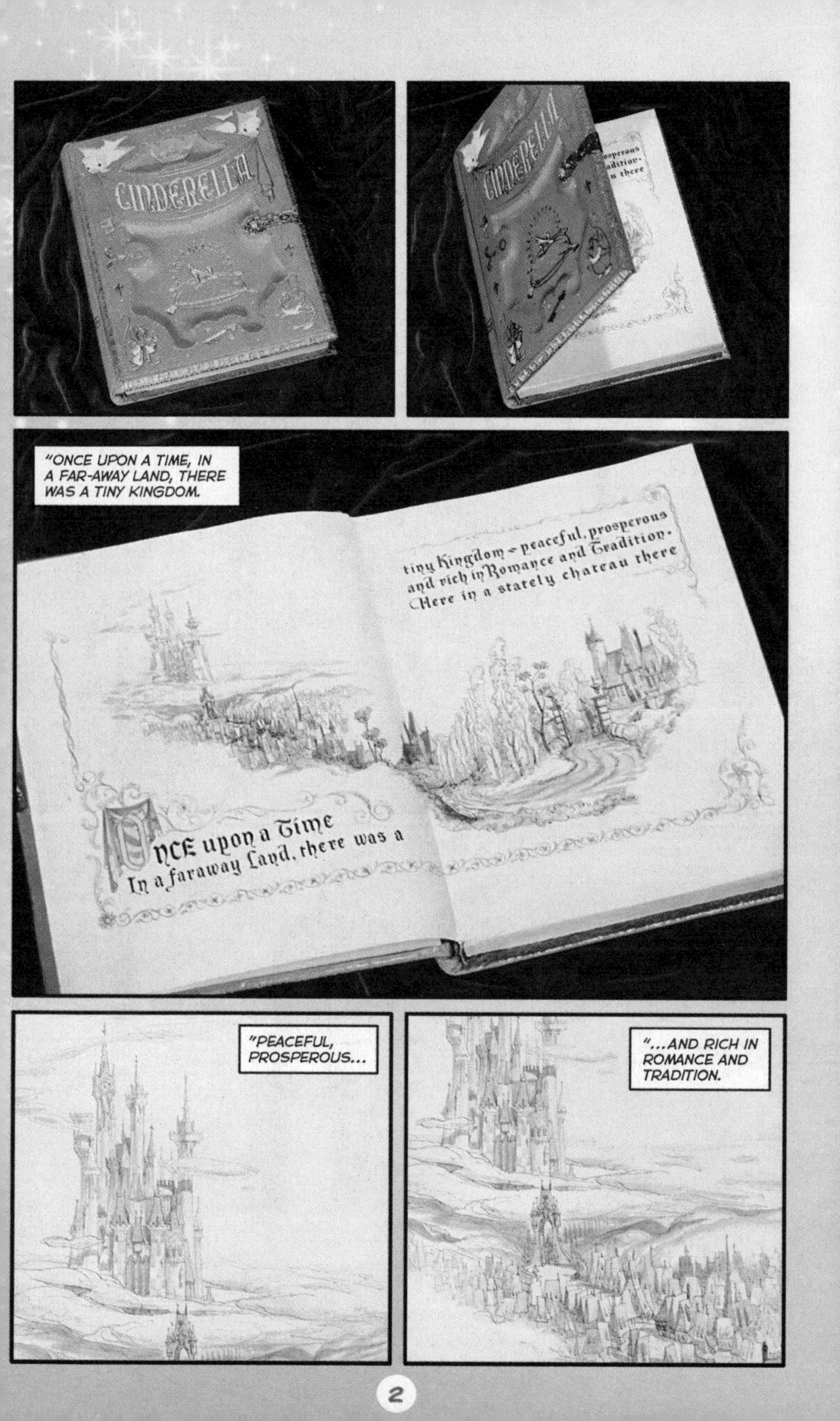

CINDERELLA
CINDERELLA
"ONCE UPON A TIME, IN A FAR-AWAY LAND, THERE WAS A TINY KINGDOM.
ONCE upon a Time
In a faraway Land, there was a
tiny Kingdom - peaceful, prosperous
and rich in Romance and Tradition.
Here in a stately chateau there
"PEACEFUL, PROSPEROUS...
"...AND RICH IN ROMANCE AND TRADITION.

"HERE, IN A STATELY CHATEAU, THERE LIVED A WIDOWED GENTLEMAN...
"...AND HIS LITTLE DAUGHTER, CINDERELLA.
"ALTHOUGH HE WAS A KIND AND DEVOTED FATHER, AND GAVE HIS BELOVED CHILD EVERY LUXURY AND COMFORT...
"...STILL HE FELT SHE NEEDED A MOTHER'S CARE."

"...AND SO HE
MARRIED AGAIN.
"CHOOSING FOR HIS SECOND
WIFE A WOMAN OF GOOD FAMILY,
WITH TWO DAUGHTERS JUST
CINDERELLA'S AGE...
"BY NAME,
ANASTASIA --
"-- AND
DRIZELLA.

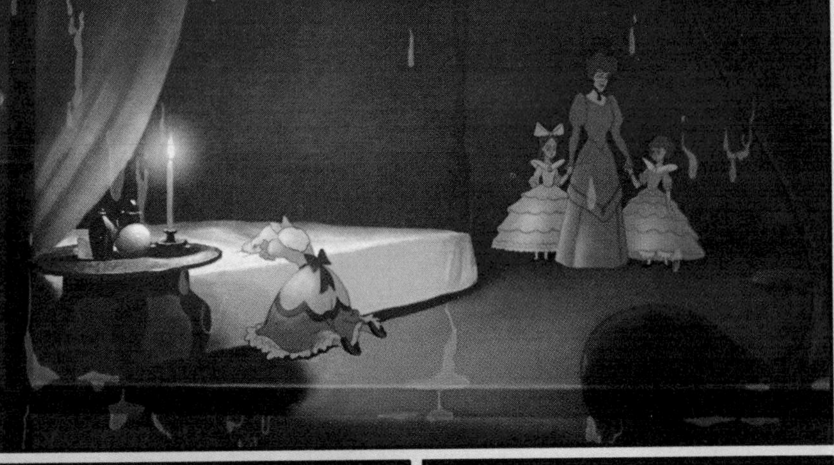

"...AND BITTERLY JEALOUS OF CINDERELLA'S CHARM AND BEAUTY...

"SHE WAS GRIMLY DETERMINED TO FORWARD THE INTERESTS OF HER OWN TWO AWKWARD DAUGHTERS.

THUS, AS TIME WENT BY, THE CHATEAU FELL INTO DISREPAIR AS THE FAMILY FORTUNES WERE SQUANDERED UPON THE VAIN AND SELFISH STEPSISTERS.
MEANWHILE, CINDERELLA WAS ABUSED, HUMILIATED...
...AND FINALLY FORCED TO BECOME A SERVANT IN HER OWN HOUSE.
AND YET, THROUGH IT ALL, CINDERELLA REMAINED EVER GENTLE AND KIND...

FOR WITH EACH DAWN SHE FOUND NEW HOPE THAT SOMEDAY...
...HER DREAMS OF HAPPINESS WOULD COME TRUE.
CINDERELLA!
CINDERELLA!
CINDERELLA!, WAKE UP!

YAWN
SHE WON'T WAKE UP!
WE'LL JUST HAVE TO TRY AGAIN!
MR. AND MRS. BLUEBIRD CHIRPED AND SANG...
BUT STILL, CINDERELLA STAYED IN BED!

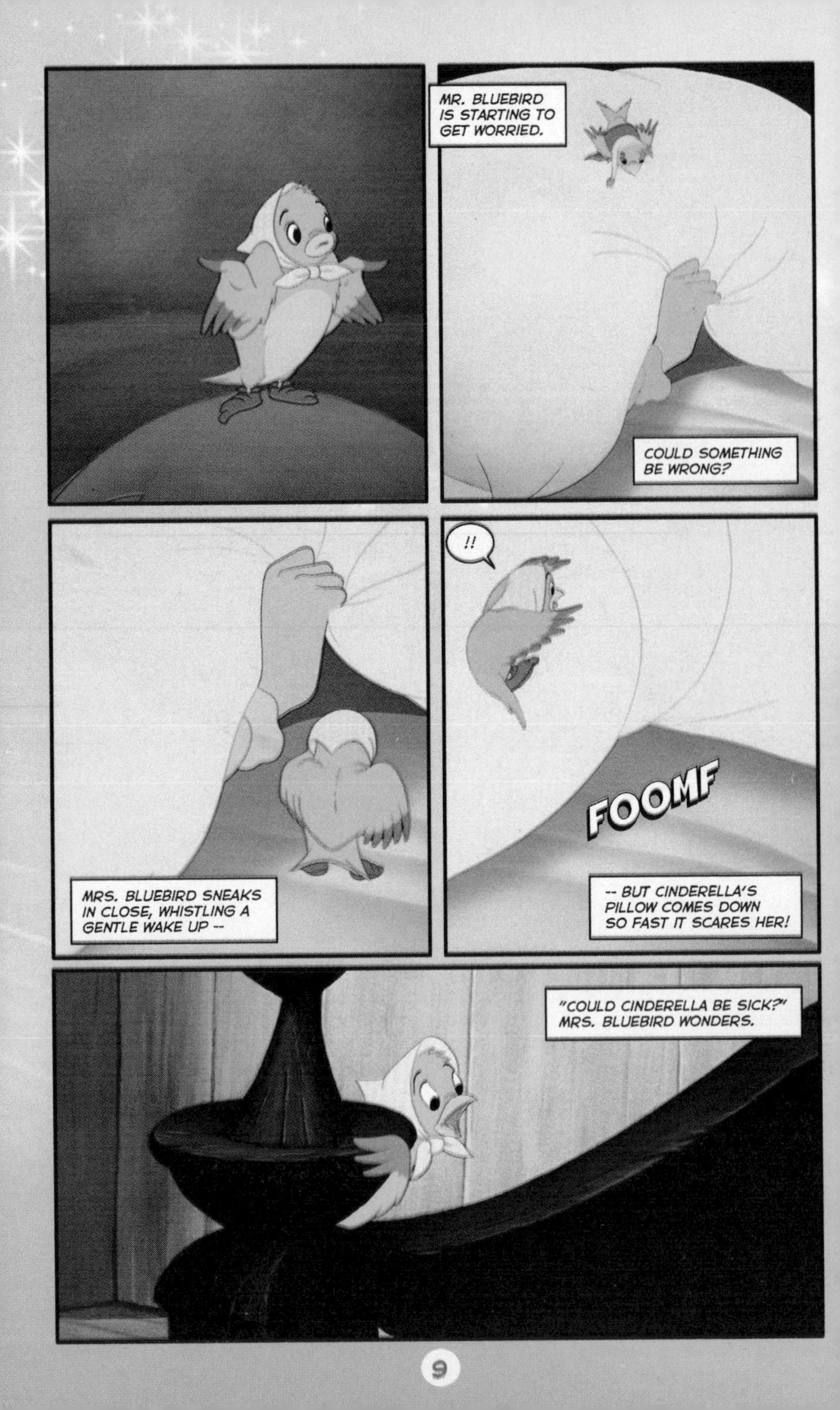
MR. BLUEBIRD
IS STARTING TO
GET WORRIED.
COULD SOMETHING
BE WRONG?
MRS. BLUEBIRD SNEAKS
IN CLOSE, WHISTLING A
GENTLE WAKE UP --
!!
FOOMF
-- BUT CINDERELLA'S
PILLOW COMES DOWN
SO FAST IT SCARES HER!
"COULD CINDERELLA BE SICK?"
MRS. BLUEBIRD WONDERS.

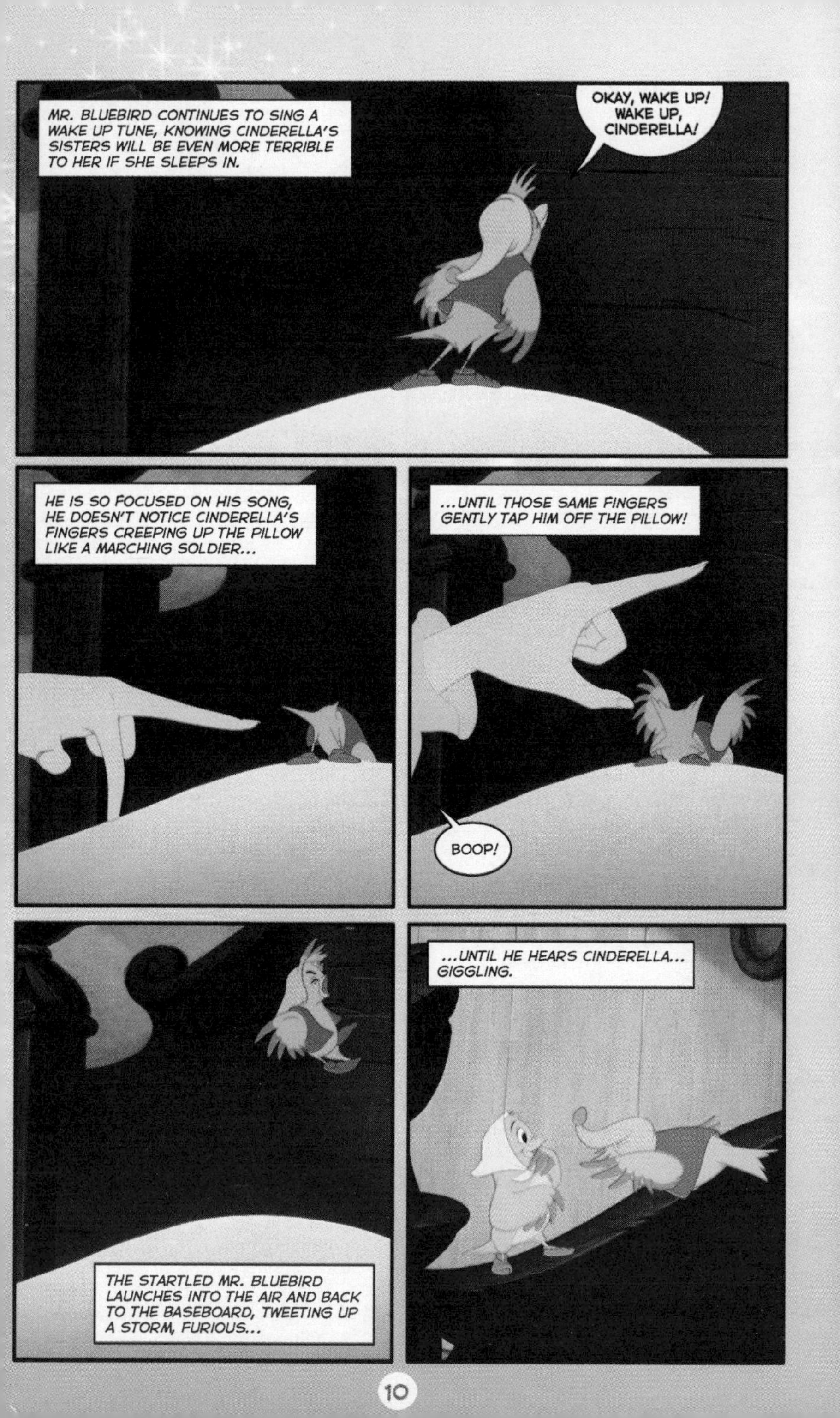
MR. BLUEBIRD CONTINUES TO SING A WAKE UP TUNE, KNOWING CINDERELLA'S SISTERS WILL BE EVEN MORE TERRIBLE TO HER IF SHE SLEEPS IN.
OKAY, WAKE UP! WAKE UP, CINDERELLA!
HE IS SO FOCUSED ON HIS SONG, HE DOESN'T NOTICE CINDERELLA'S FINGERS CREEPING UP THE PILLOW LIKE A MARCHING SOLDIER...
...UNTIL THOSE SAME FINGERS GENTLY TAP HIM OFF THE PILLOW!
BOOP!
THE STARTLED MR. BLUEBIRD LAUNCHES INTO THE AIR AND BACK TO THE BASEBOARD, TWEETING UP A STORM, FURIOUS...
...UNTIL HE HEARS CINDERELLA... GIGGLING.

HA HAHA!
WELL IT SERVES YOU RIGHT -- SPOILING OTHER PEOPLE'S BEST DREAMS.
MR. BLUEBIRD FORGETS HIS MOMENTARY GRUMPINESS AS MRS. BLUEBIRD CHEERFULLY TWEETS TO CINDERELLA...
AND THEN TOGETHER, THE BLUEBIRDS FLY TO THE WINDOW...
...TO POINT OUT A MOST BEAUTIFUL SUNRISE.
TWEET!
YES, I KNOW IT'S A LOVELY MORNING,

...BUT IT WAS A LOVELY DREAM, TOO.

SIGH

WHAT KIND OF DREAM?

MM-MM. I CAN'T TELL.

WHY?
BECAUSE IF YOU TELL A WISH, IT WON'T COME TRUE.

AND AFTER ALL...

A DREAM IS A WISH YOUR HEART MAKES.
IT IS?
OH, YES.
YES, BECAUSE YOUR DREAMS ARE ALWAYS WAITING FOR YOU...
...WHEN YOU LEAVE YOUR DAY BEHIND.

HEARING CINDERELLA'S VOICE, MORE BIRDS FLY IN TO WISH HER GOOD MORNING.
SOME MORE ENTHUSIASTICALLY THAN OTHERS.
TWEET TWEEET ♫♫
MMPH!
SHH!
HMPH.
THERE'S NO ONE THERE TO STOP YOU...
...OR TO TAKE IT AWAY FROM YOU.

TWEET-TWEEEEEET! ♫♫
IT'S TRUE!
WHEN YOU KNOW WHAT YOUR HEART WANTS...
...YOU CAN WORK TO MAKE IT HAPPEN IN REAL LIFE.

ZZZ---
SNRT.
WHATS?
IS CINDERELLY TALKING ABOUT DREAMS?
YAWWWN. MUST BE TIME TO WAKE UP.
TSK.
...STUPID SNAG INNA TAIL.

COULD MY DREAMS COME TRUE, CINDERELLY?
OF COURSE, JAQ!
BUT FIRST YOU MUST KNOW WHAT YOUR HEART TRULY WANTS.
THEN YOU MUST HAVE FAITH AND GOOD INTENTIONS...
...AND WORK FOR WHAT YOU BELIEVE IN.
BONG

BONG
OH, THAT CLOCK!
BONG
OLD KILLJOY.
I HEAR YOU!
"COME ON, GET UP," YOU SAY! "TIME TO START ANOTHER DAY!"
EVEN HE ORDERS ME AROUND!

BUT THERE'S ONE THING --
-- THEY CAN'T GET ME TO STOP DREAMING.
AND PERHAPS SOMEDAY...
...WITH A LITTLE LUCK...
...MY HEART WILL FIND WHAT IT WANTS.

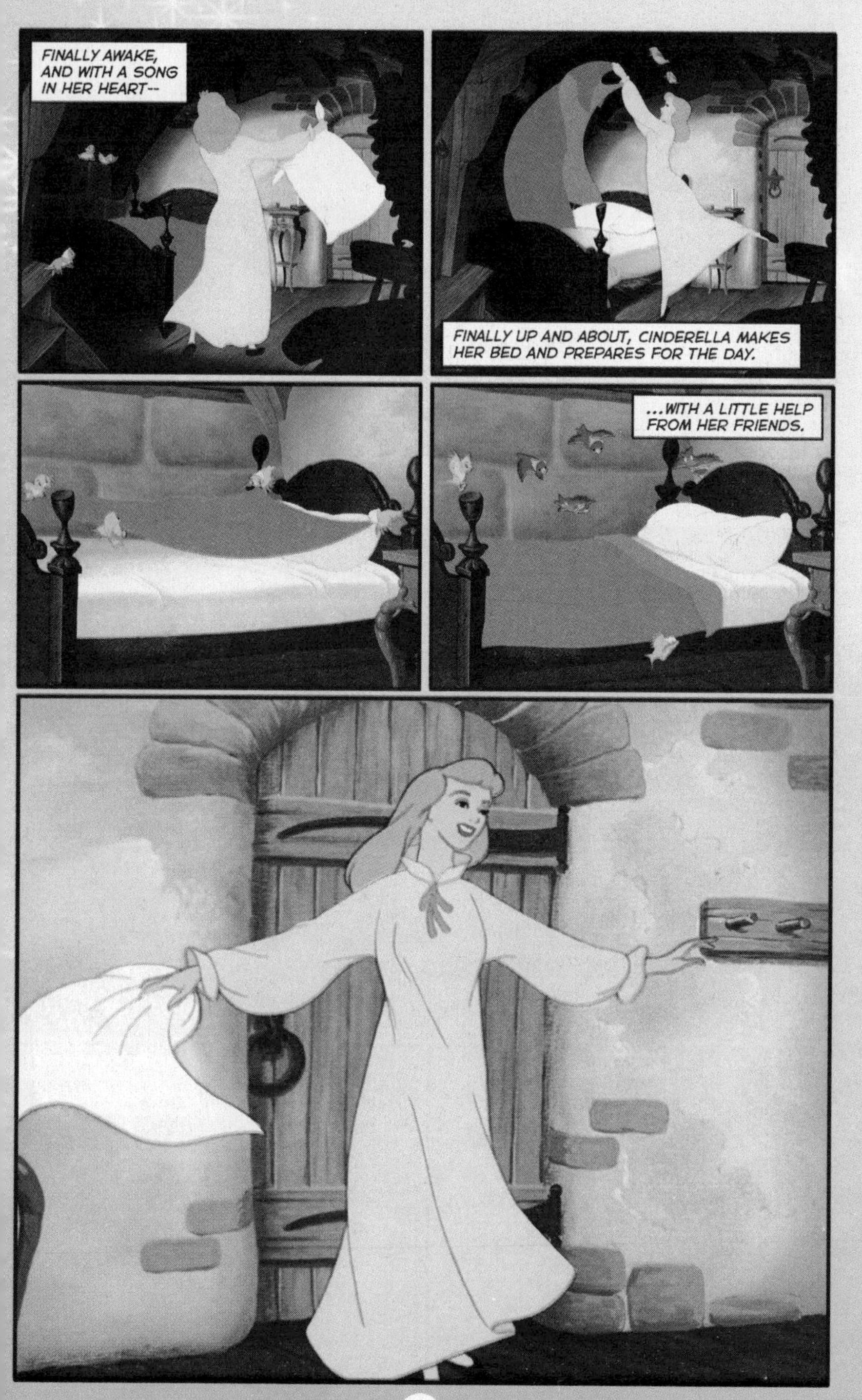
FINALLY AWAKE, AND WITH A SONG IN HER HEART--
FINALLY UP AND ABOUT, CINDERELLA MAKES HER BED AND PREPARES FOR THE DAY.
...WITH A LITTLE HELP FROM HER FRIENDS.

SHOO! SHOO! GET OUT OF HERE!
THE MICE POUR A BASIN OF WATER...
CAREFUL, CAREFUL--!
SPLASH
...THEN THE BIRDS COLLECT IT WITH A SPONGE...

...TO HELP GIVE CINDERELLA A QUICK WASHING.
squishhhh
...BRR!
THE WASHING DONE, THE BIRDS LAY OUT CINDERELLA'S DRESS --
-- AND HER APRON! --

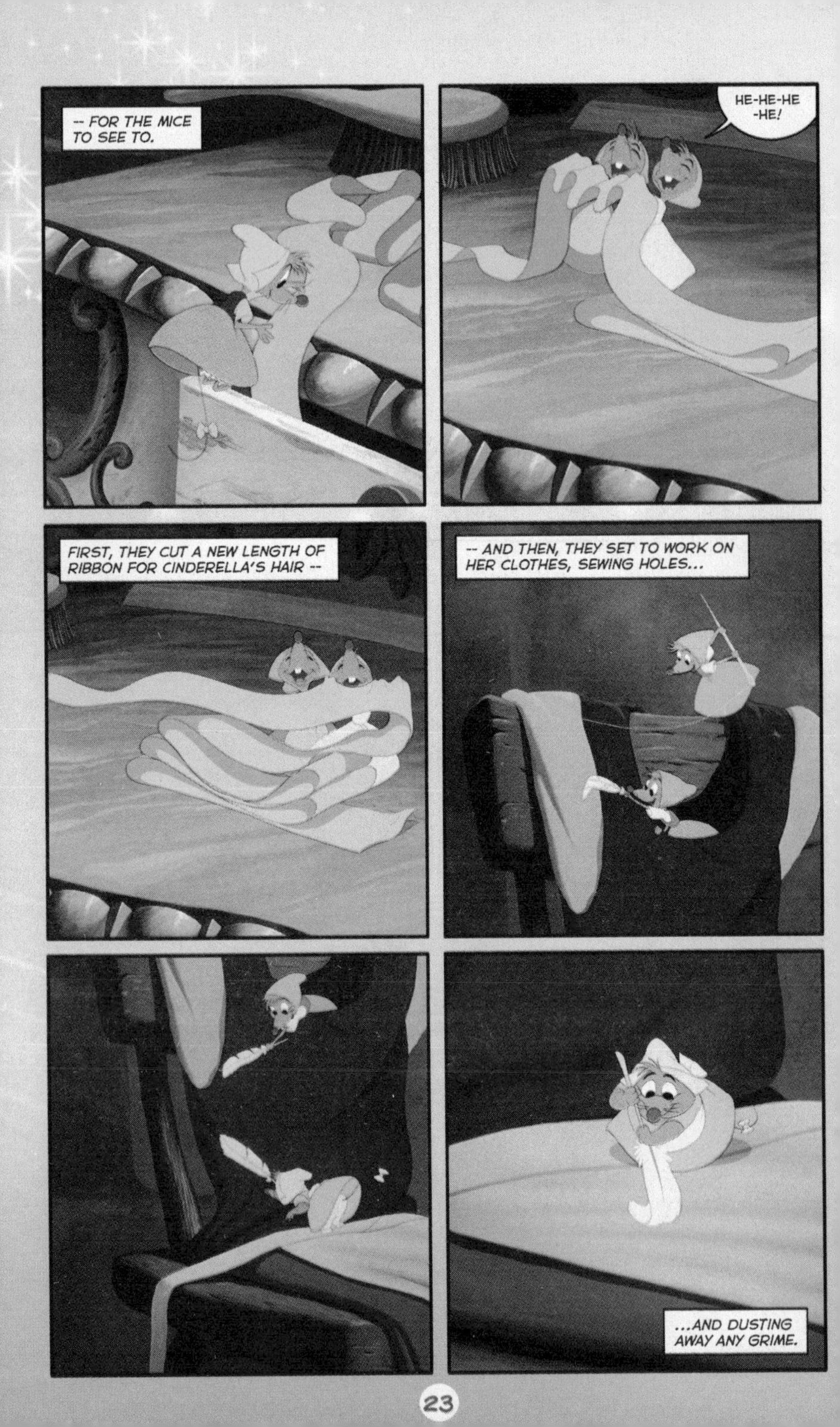
-- FOR THE MICE
TO SEE TO.
HE-HE-HE
-HE!
FIRST, THEY CUT A NEW LENGTH OF
RIBBON FOR CINDERELLA'S HAIR --
-- AND THEN, THEY SET TO WORK ON
HER CLOTHES, SEWING HOLES...
...AND DUSTING
AWAY ANY GRIME.

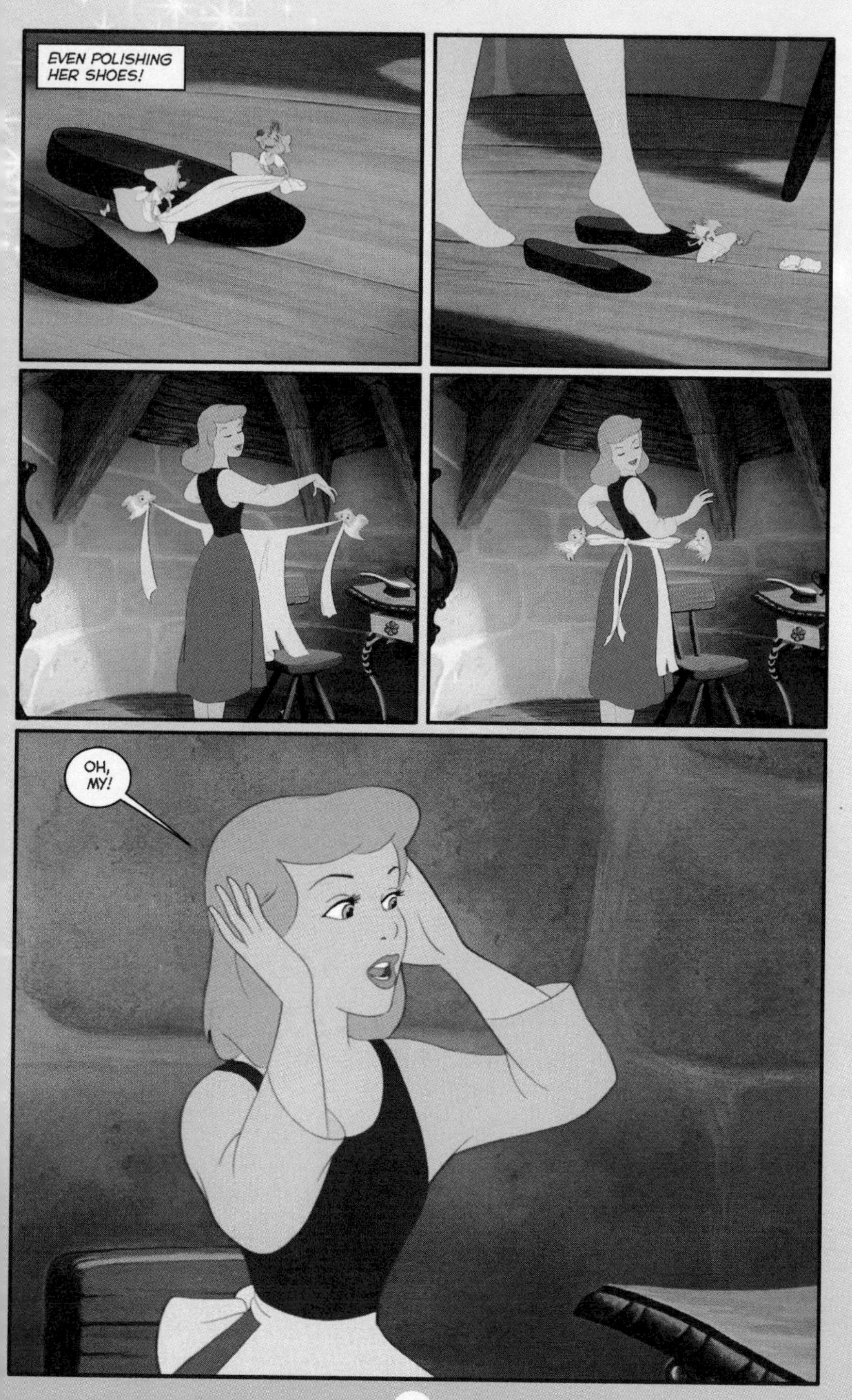
EVEN POLISHING HER SHOES!
OH, MY!

IS THAT RIBBON FOR ME?
THANK YOU SO MUCH.
IT REALLY IS A LOVELY SHADE OF BLUE.
JUST LIKE YOU TWO!

THERE. ALL READY.
C'MON, C'MON, C'MON...
WAIT! WAIT!
NOPE, NOPE, NO WAIT, C'MON...
WAIT!
WAIT A MINUTE, WAIT A MINUTE...
ONE AT A TIME, PLEASE.

NOW, JAQ -- WHAT'S ALL THE FUSS ABOUT?
NEW MOUSE IN THE HOUSE! BRAND NEW!
NEVER SAW BEFORE! VISITOR! VISITOR!
OH, A VISITOR.
WELL, SHE'LL NEED A DRESS...

HAHAHA HAHA!
NO, NO, NO!
NOT A SHE - A HE!
OH. THAT DOES MAKE A DIFFERENCE.
HE'LL NEED A JACKET, AND SHOES...
GOTTA GET HIM OUT! TRAP! IN A TRAP!
WHERE? IN A TRAP?

WELL, WHY DIDN'T YOU SAY SO?
AS FAST AS SHE CAN, CINDERELLA AND THE MICE RACE FROM HER ATTIC ROOM...
...DOWN DOZENS OF STEPS...
...TO THE TRAP AND ITS CAPTURED MOUSE.

NOW, NOW, NOW
CALM DOWN,
EVERYBODY.
OH!
THE POOR LITTLE
THING'S SCARED
TO DEATH.
JAQ, MAYBE YOU'D
BETTER EXPLAIN
THINGS TO
HIM.
ZUK ZUK,
CINDERELLY.
ZUK ZUK.

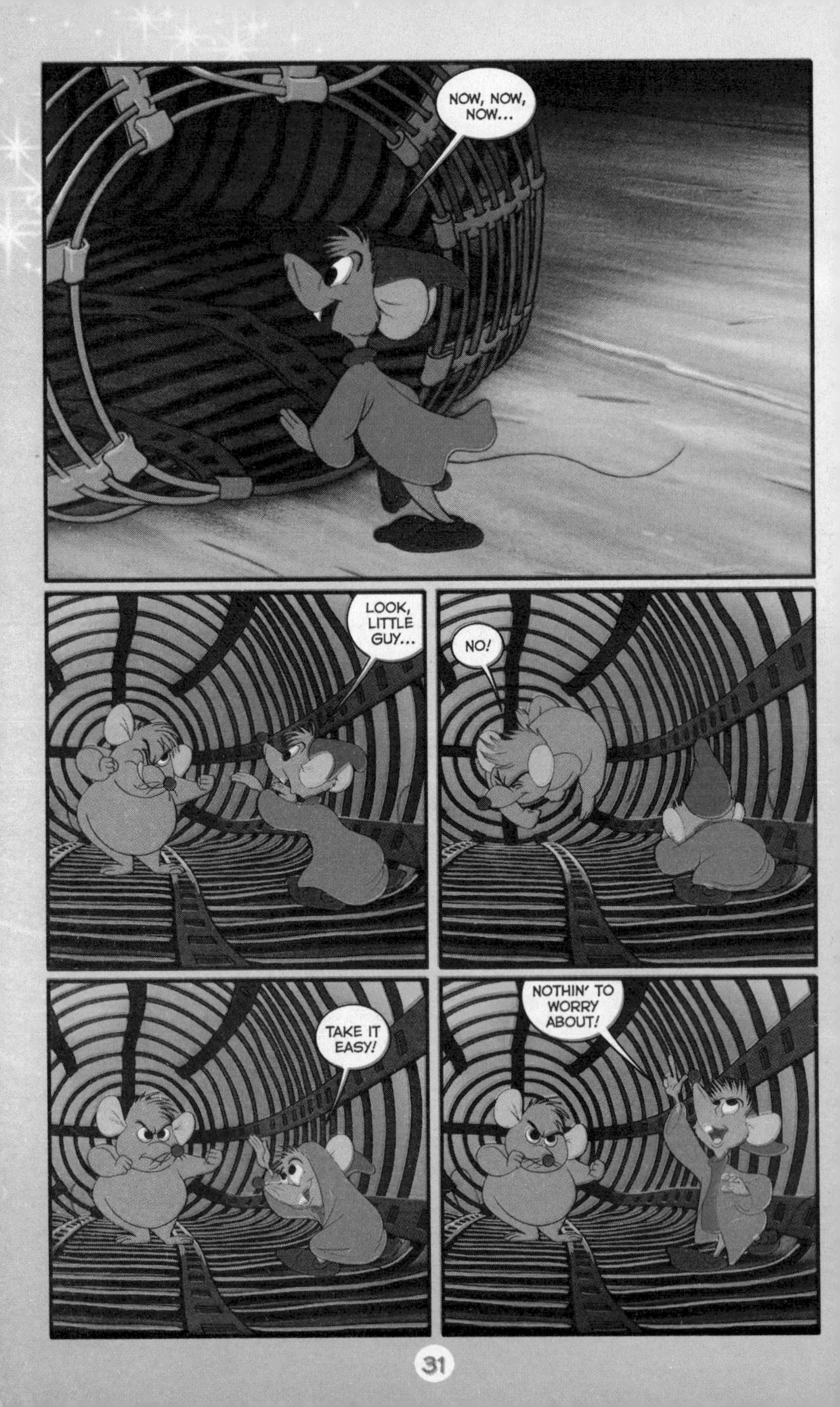
NOW, NOW, NOW...
LOOK, LITTLE GUY...
NO!
TAKE IT EASY!
NOTHIN' TO WORRY ABOUT!

WE LIKE YOU!
CINDERELLY LIKES YOU, TOO!
SHE'S NICE -- VERY NICE!
THAT'S BETTER!
C'MON, NOW -- ZUK ZUK ZUK!
WELL, THAT'S BETTER!

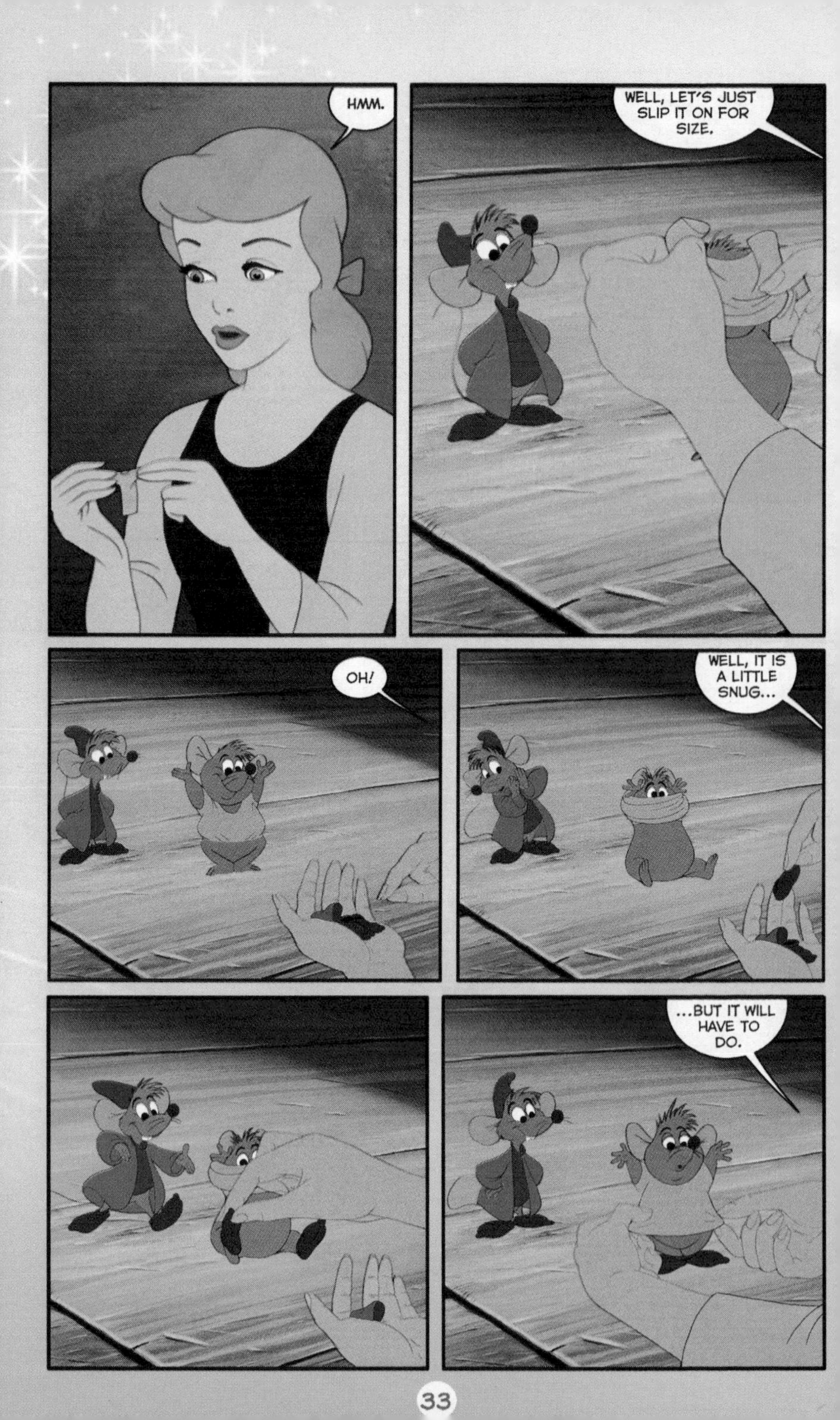

HMM.
WELL, LET'S JUST SLIP IT ON FOR SIZE.
OH!
WELL, IT IS A LITTLE SNUG...
...BUT IT WILL HAVE TO DO.

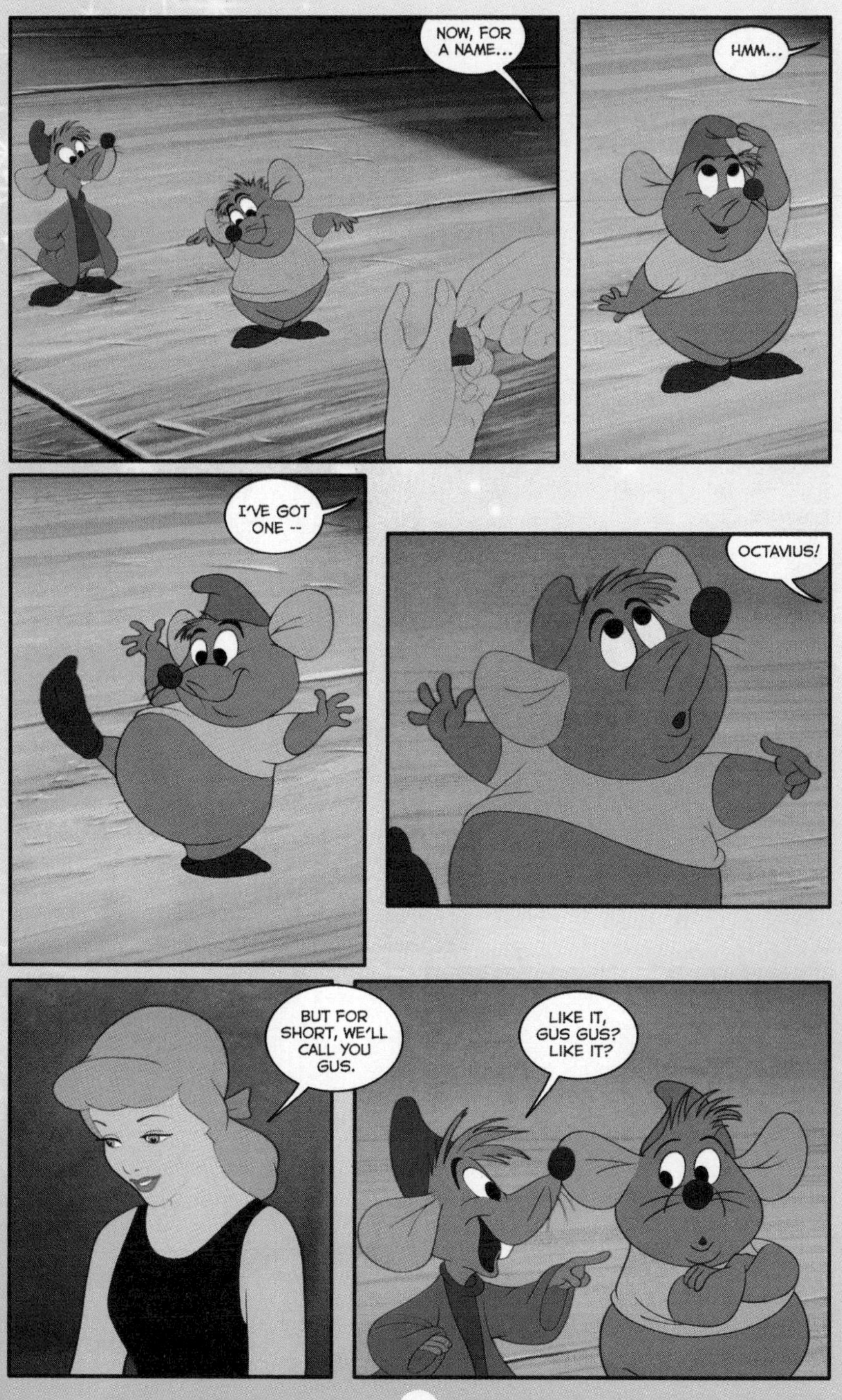
NOW, FOR A NAME...
HMM...
I'VE GOT ONE --
OCTAVIUS!
BUT FOR SHORT, WE'LL CALL YOU GUS.
LIKE IT, GUS GUS? LIKE IT?

UH...GUS GUS - HA HA! YEAH.
NOW I'VE GOT TO HURRY.
SEE THAT HE KEEPS OUT OF TROUBLE, JAQ.
AND DON'T FORGET TO WARN HIM ABOUT THE CAT.
ZUK ZUK!
LOOK, AH -- EVER SEE A CAT-CAT?

UH, CAT-CAT?
YUP, CAT-CAT!
LUCIFER! I'LL TELL YOU.
MEAN. SNEAKY.
JUMP AT YOU!

BITE AT YOU!
BIG AS A HOUSE!
MEEEOOOWWW!
ZUK ZUK -- LUCIFEE?
DUUUH LUCIFEE.
ZUK ZUK!

LEAVING THE MICE BEHIND, CINDERELLA QUIETLY MAKES HER WAY DOWN TO THE MAIN PART OF THE CHATEAU...
...QUIETLY SHUTTING THE DOOR BEHIND HER SO AS NOT TO WAKEN ANYONE TOO SUDDENLY.
CINDERELLA OPENS THE WIDE CURTAINS TO LET IN THE SUNLIGHT...
...AND SOFTLY WALKS TO HER STEPMOTHER'S BEDROOM DOOR...

...WHERE SHE CAN HEAR THE SOUND OF SNORING...
...MIXED WITH PURRING.
HER STEPMOTHER'S PRECIOUS CAT:
LUCIFER.
MRRROW?

YAWN.
COME, KITTY. COME ON.
YAAAAWN.
LUCIFER LOOKS AT CINDERELLA AS THOUGH SHE WASN'T SOMETHING WORTH WAKING UP FOR.
AND THEN, PERHAPS DECIDING THIS IS THE CASE, HE TURNS HIS BACK ON CINDERELLA...
...AND CURLS BACK UP INTO HIS BED.

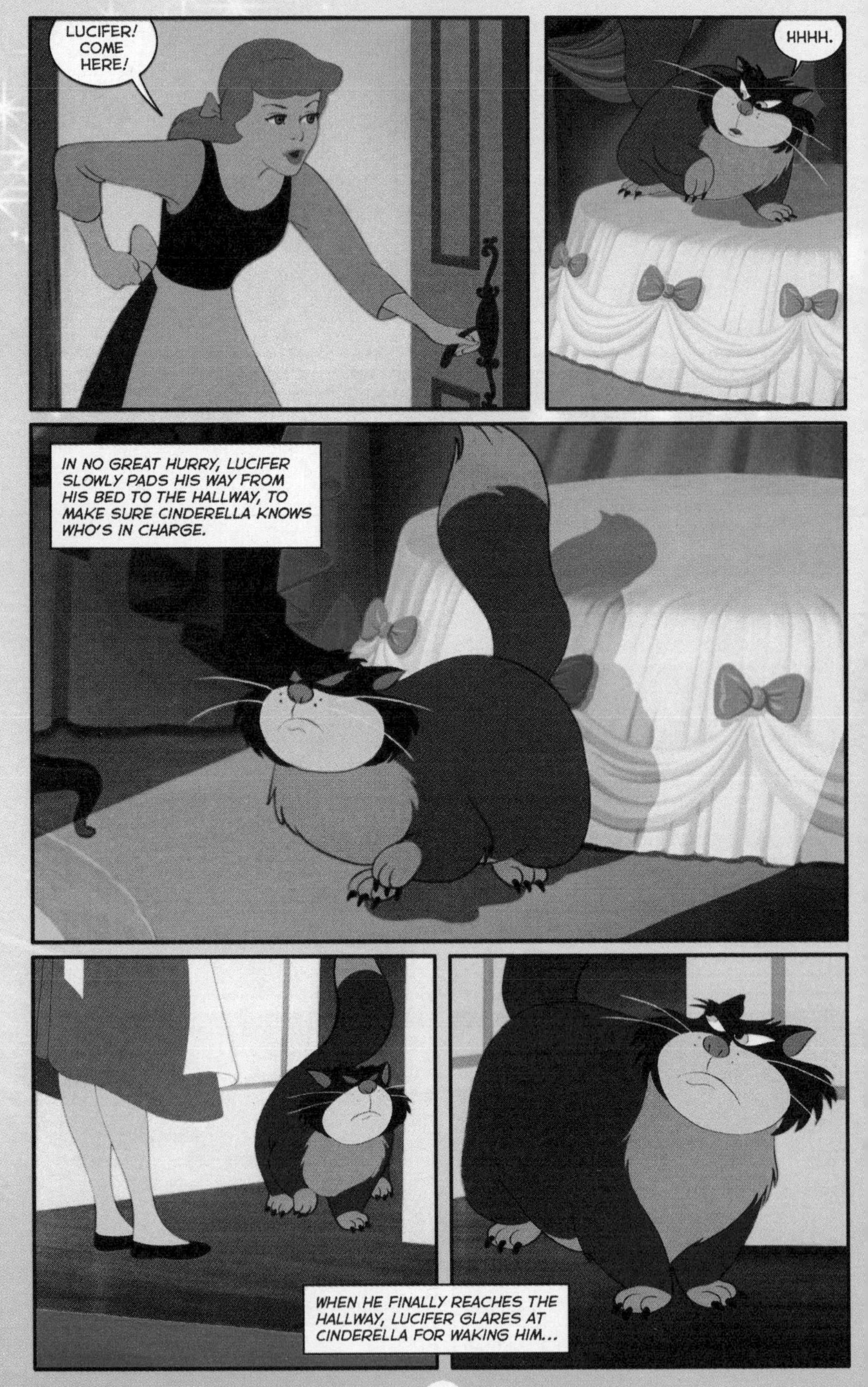
LUCIFER! COME HERE!
HHHH.
IN NO GREAT HURRY, LUCIFER SLOWLY PADS HIS WAY FROM HIS BED TO THE HALLWAY, TO MAKE SURE CINDERELLA KNOWS WHO'S IN CHARGE.
WHEN HE FINALLY REACHES THE HALLWAY, LUCIFER GLARES AT CINDERELLA FOR WAKING HIM...

YAAAWN.
skritch
skritch
...AND THEN SCRATCHES UP THE FLOOR TO MAKE SURE SHE KNOWS HE'S NOT HAPPY.
CINDERELLA CLOSES THE BEDROOM DOOR, KNOCKING LUCIFER OFF BALANCE TO STOP THE SCRATCHING.
'IF ONLY SHE WERE A MOUSE,' HE THINKS,'I'D SWALLOW HER WHOLE.'
I'M SORRY IF YOUR HIGHNESS OBJECTS TO AN EARLY BREAKFAST.
SEE?

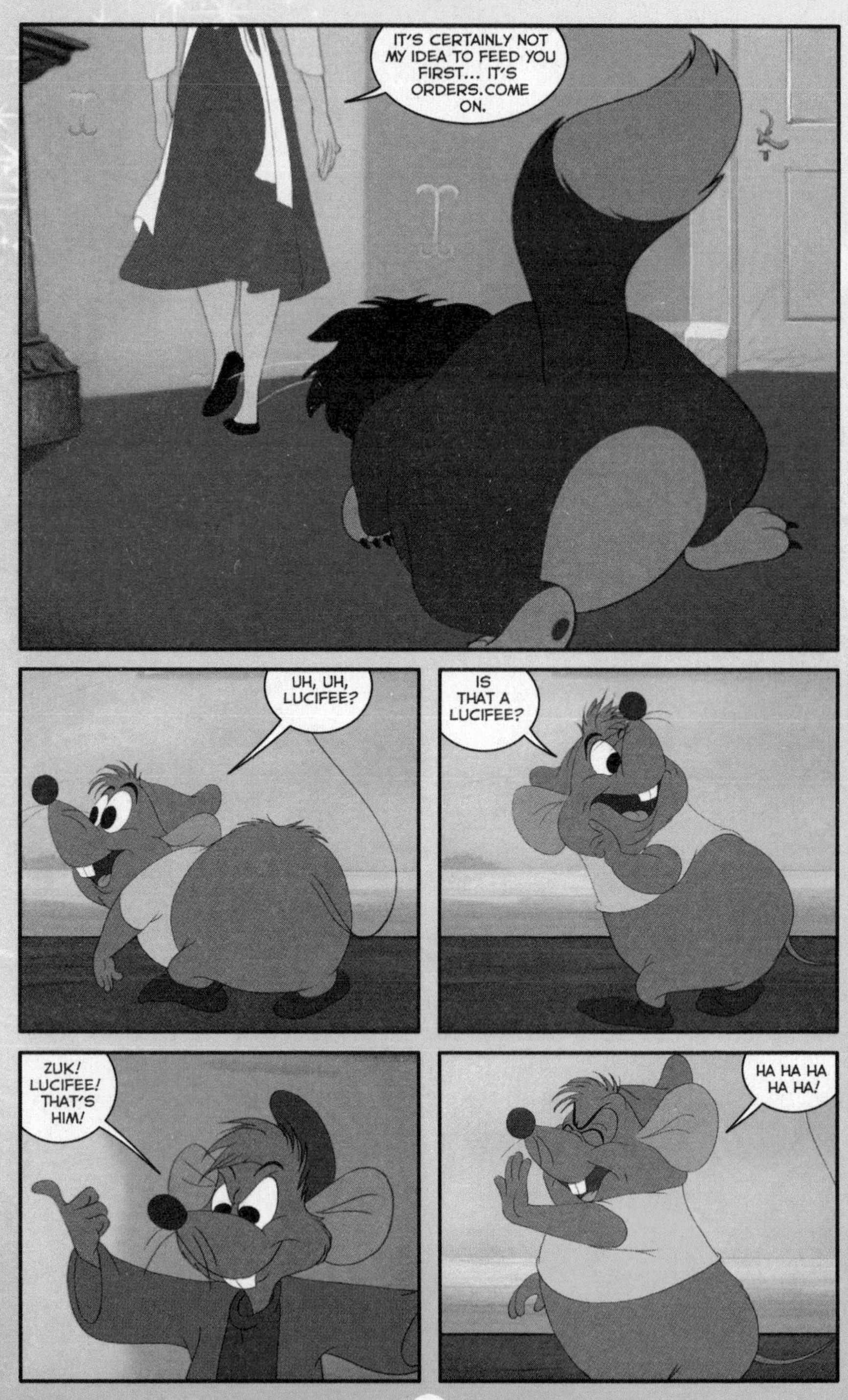
IT'S CERTAINLY NOT MY IDEA TO FEED YOU FIRST... IT'S ORDERS. COME ON.
UH, UH, LUCIFEE?
IS THAT A LUCIFEE?
ZUK! LUCIFEE! THAT'S HIM!
HA HA HA HA HA!

GUS-GUS TAKE A LUCIFEE AND -- KRRRRRRK!
LOOKIT!
NO, GUS-GUS, NO!
NOW LISTEN HERE -- LUCIFEE NOT FUNNY.
LUCIFEE MEAN.

MEANWHILE, AS JAQ FILLS GUS' HEAD WITH STORIES OF LUCIFER'S MEANNESS, CINDERELLA HAS REACHED THE KITCHEN.
LUCIFER IS READY FOR HIS BREAKFAST NOW, BUT THE SOUNDS OF A CERTAIN SOMEONE FOUL HIS MOOD.
WOOF... SNORE...
HSSSS.
WOOOF... SNORE...
YIP! YIP! YIP!
BRUNO...

GRRR-ARF! ARF!
BRUNO!
GRR! GRRR---
SNORT...
DREAMING AGAIN.

CHASING LUCIFER?
CATCH HIM THIS TIME? THAT'S --
--BAD!
HEH HEH HEH HEH HEH.
SUPPOSE THEY HEARD YOU UPSTAIRS!

YOU KNOW THE ORDERS!
SO IF YOU DON'T WANT TO LOSE A NICE, WARM BED --
-- YOU'D BETTER GET RID OF THOSE DREAMS!
KNOW HOW?
?

JUST LEARN TO LIKE CATS!
BLEH!

NO, I MEAN IT!

LUCIFER HAS HIS GOOD POINTS, TOO.

FOR ONE THING, HE --

UM...
WELL, SOMETIMES, HE --
-- HM.
THERE MUST BE SOMETHING GOOD ABOUT HIM.
SNORT!

HA HA
HA!

SNORT.
GIGGLE.
CINDERELLA WAS WRONG. THERE IS NOTHING GOOD ABOUT LUCIFER... BUT THAT DOESN'T MEAN HE'S JUST GOING TO LET BRUNO LAUGH ABOUT IT.

NOW, HE WONDERS, WHAT WOULD BE THE BEST WAY TO TAKE REVENGE?

LUCIFER KNOWS RIGHT AWAY WHAT TO DO.

WHILE BRUNO IS LAUGHING, LUCIFER LAYS DOWN IN FRONT OF HIM...
...SPRINGS HIS CLAWS, AND...
YIPE!
SLASH!
GRRRRR---

SNARL!
MEOW!!
BRUNO!
OH, BRUNO. COME ON, NOW.
OUTSIDE.

LUCIFER SMILES. HIS TRICK HAD WORKED...
...AND BRUNO WAS BANISHED TO THE YARD.
MAYBE THAT WOULD TEACH THE OLD DOG WHO WAS BOSS.
OH, I KNOW IT ISN'T EASY...
...BUT AT LEAST WE SHOULD TRY TO GET ALONG TOGETHER.

AND THAT INCLUDES YOU...
"...YOUR MAJESTY."
LUCIFER'S GOOD MOOD WAS SPOILED.
SHE HAD BEEN RUDE TO HIM. TO HIM!
IF ONLY SHE HAD BEEN A MOUSE - THEN HE WOULD SHOW HER.
IF ONLY.

BREAKFAST TIME!
BREAKFAST TIME!
EVERYBODY UP!
HURRY! HURRY!

COME ON, EVERYBODY!
BREAKFAST! BREAKFAST!
BREAKFAST?
COME ON, LET'S EAT!
HA HA HA HA! WAIT, BREAKFAST?

OH!

BREAKFAST!!

CHEERFULLY, THE MICE SCAMPER DOWN THE INSIDES OF THE CHATEAU WALLS...

MAKING THEIR WAY TOWARDS THAT MOST MAGICAL OF THINGS --

--A FREE MEAL.

JAQ LEADS THE WAY, RACING
AHEAD OF THE OTHER MICE...
HE'S SO EXCITED FOR BREAKFAST,
HE ALMOST RUNS RIGHT INTO THE
WORST KIND OF TROUBLE!
UH-OH!

-- LUCIFEE!
HOW WE GONNA GET OUT?
QUICKLY, THE MICE SCAMPER BACK INTO THE SAFETY OF THE CHATEAU WALLS.
WELL, MOST OF THEM.
GUS-GUS!

ZUK ZUK
CAREFUL!
WITH THEIR PATH TO BREAKFAST BLOCKED, JAQ STARTS THINKING AS HARD AS HE CAN.
HOW WILL THEY PASS THE DREADED LUCIFER WITHOUT BECOMING BREAKFAST THEMSELVES?

GOT IT!
OKAY, EVERYBODY --
I GOT AN IDEA.
SO LISTEN UP!

NOW, SOMEBODY GOTTA SNEAK OUT --
-- GET LUCIFER TO CHASE THEM.
THEN RUN OVER TO A CORNER... AND KEEP HIM THERE.
THEN, WE ALL RUN OUT. ZUK?
ZUK ZUK! OUT!

NOW WE CHOOSE WHO GOTTA DO IT.
EVERYBODY, HUP!
HUP!
DUH, HUP!

TAILS UP!
HUP!
HUP!
NOW!
HUP! HUP! HUP!

UH... HUP!
JAQ HAS SELECTED THE TAIL OF THE MOUSE THAT HAS TO FACE OFF AGAINST LUCIFER.
HE OPENS HIS EYES, WONDERING WHO THE UNLUCKY MOUSE WOULD BE.
AND THEN REALIZES...
HE'S HOLDING HIS OWN TAIL.

GUS, THINKING JAQ HAS WON, OFFERS A HANDSHAKE IN CONGRATULATIONS.
THE OTHER MICE, WHO ALL KNOW LUCIFER BETTER, WAVE GOODBYE...
...AS IF HE WON'T BE COMING BACK.
ZUK!

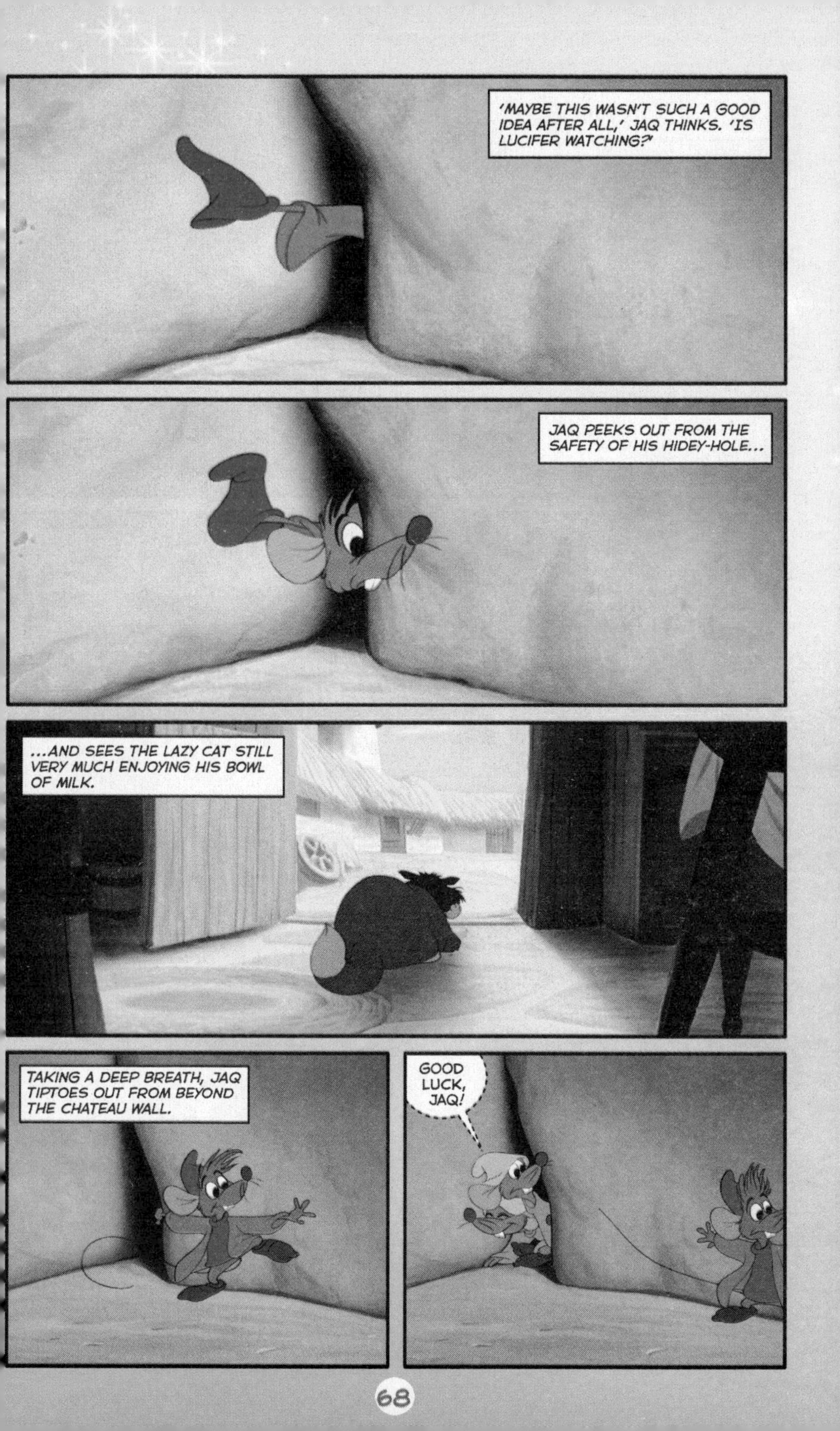
'MAYBE THIS WASN'T SUCH A GOOD IDEA AFTER ALL,' JAQ THINKS. 'IS LUCIFER WATCHING?'
JAQ PEEKS OUT FROM THE SAFETY OF HIS HIDEY-HOLE...
...AND SEES THE LAZY CAT STILL VERY MUCH ENJOYING HIS BOWL OF MILK.
TAKING A DEEP BREATH, JAQ TIPTOES OUT FROM BEYOND THE CHATEAU WALL.
GOOD LUCK, JAQ!

SLOWLY, JAQ CREEPS ALONG THE WALL...
CLOSER AND CLOSER TO LUCIFER.
HE CAN'T MAKE A SOUND.
NOT A SINGLE SOUND!

AS JAQ CROSSES THE FLOOR, HE SMILES.
HE HASN'T BEEN NOTICED YET!
MAYBE THIS IS BECAUSE
LUCIFER IS STILL HALF ASLEEP?
THE CAT WAS LEANING
PRETTY FAR OVER HIS
BOWL OF MILK...
...AND THAT GAVE
JAQ ANOTHER IDEA.

THE BRAVE LITTLE MOUSE WAVED TO HIS FRIENDS, TO GET THEIR ATTENTION.
WHEN HE WAS SURE THEY WERE WATCHING...
JAQ SILENTLY EXPLAINED HIS PLAN.
SINCE LUCIFER WAS PROPPED UP ON HIS ELBOW...
...JAQ WOULD KNOCK HIM OFF BALANCE WITH A WELL-PLACED KICK, AND THEN THE OTHERS COULD RUN.

THE MICE UNDERSTOOD THE PLAN.
EVEN GUS!
HAHAHA HAHA!
SHHHH!
ALL THAT WAS LEFT WAS TO PUT THE PLAN INTO ACTION.
READY...

SET...
THWACK
KR-SPLASHHH
GASP!
PTUI!

LUCIFER WIPES THE MILK FROM HIS EYE AND LOOKS- WHO WOULD BE SO FOOLISH AS TO DO THIS TO HIM?
A MOUSE!!!
LUCIFER GRINS AS HE GIVES CHASE. MAYBE IT WASN'T SUCH A TERRIBLE MORNING AFTER ALL.
FIRST HE GOT BRUNO THROWN OUT OF THE HOUSE, AND NOW --
NOW HE'LL HAVE A FRESH MOUSE TO GO WITH THE REST OF HIS MILK.

JAQ ZIGS AND ZAGS ACROSS THE KITCHEN FLOOR, WITH LUCIFER RIGHT BEHIND HIM.
CAN SEE THE SAFETY OF THE WALL... IF HE CAN REACH THE BROOM BEFORE LUCIFER JUMPS...
THUD
HAH!

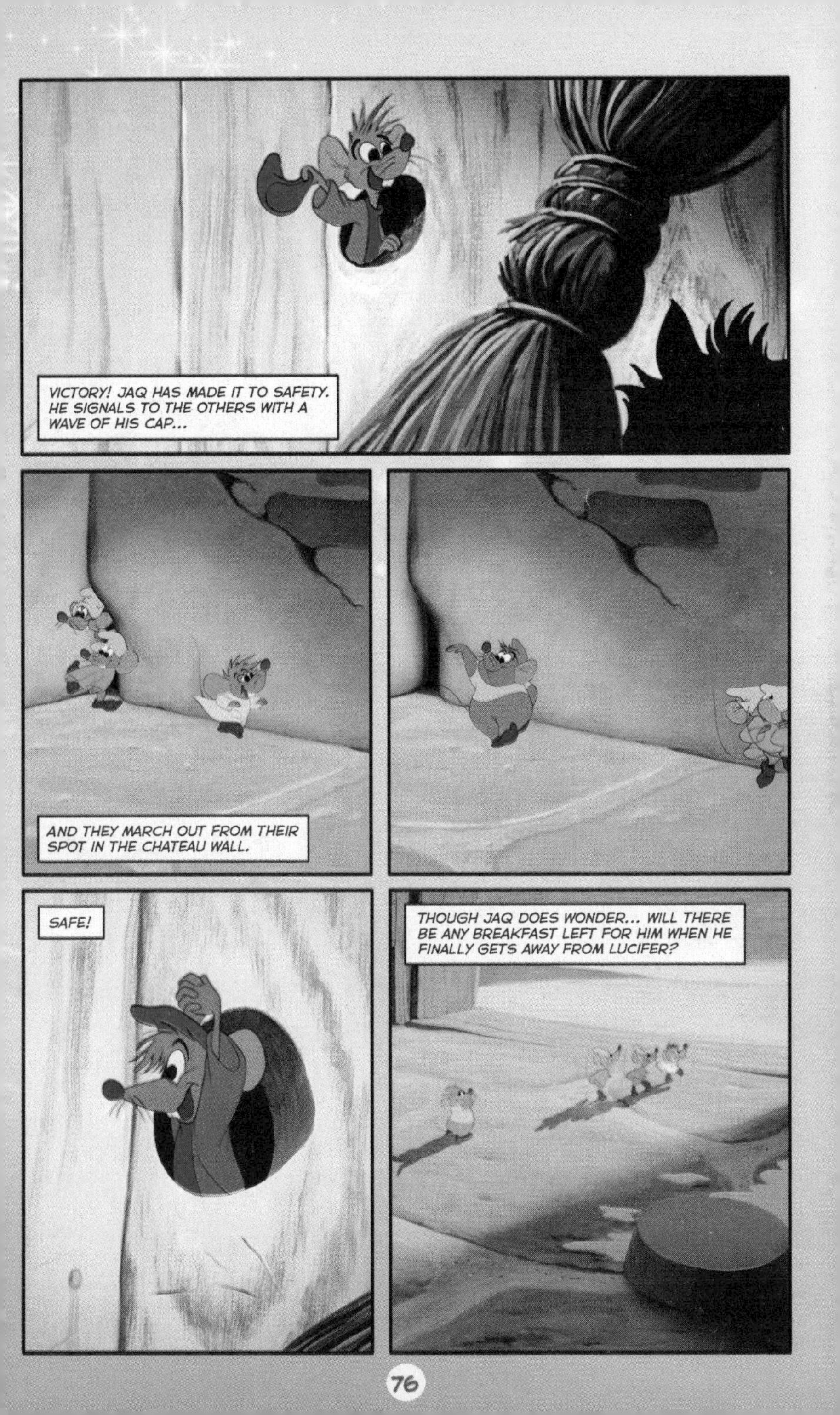
VICTORY! JAQ HAS MADE IT TO SAFETY. HE SIGNALS TO THE OTHERS WITH A WAVE OF HIS CAP...
AND THEY MARCH OUT FROM THEIR SPOT IN THE CHATEAU WALL.
SAFE!
THOUGH JAQ DOES WONDER... WILL THERE BE ANY BREAKFAST LEFT FOR HIM WHEN HE FINALLY GETS AWAY FROM LUCIFER?

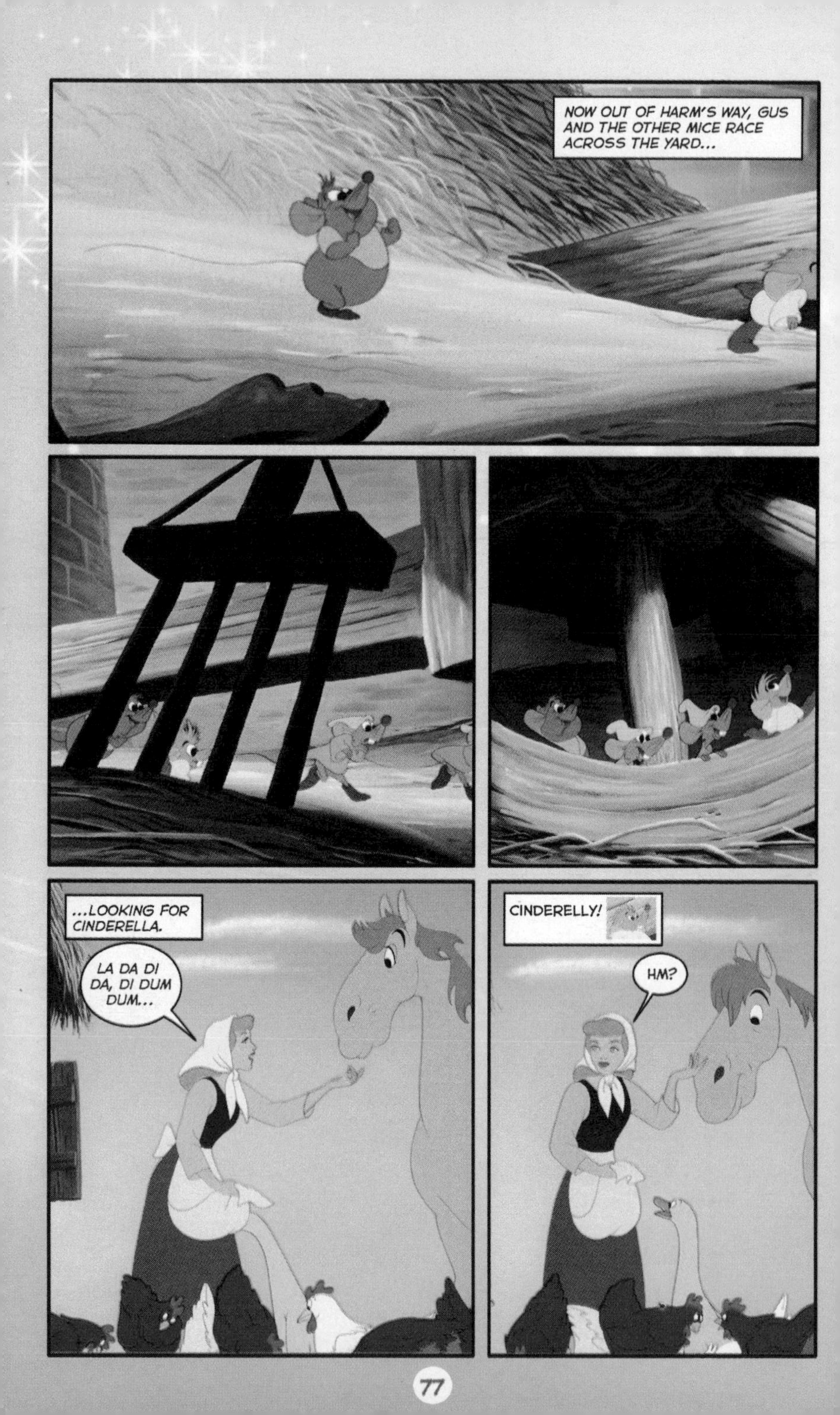
NOW OUT OF HARM'S WAY, GUS AND THE OTHER MICE RACE ACROSS THE YARD...
...LOOKING FOR CINDERELLA.
LA DA DI DA, DI DUM DUM...
CINDERELLY!
HM?

CINDERELLY, OVER HERE! CINDERELLY!
OH, THERE YOU ARE! I WAS WONDERING.
ALL RIGHT --
BREAKFAST IS SERVED.
THE OTHER MICE GRAB A KERNEL OR TWO OF CORN AND RUN OFF BEFORE THE CHICKENS CAN GET TO IT.

BUT POOR GUS ISN'T QUITE SO FAST!
...AND THE CHICKENS ARE IN NO MOOD TO SHARE.
THEY GOBBLE UP THE CORN FEED SO QUICKLY. SOON THERE'S JUST ONE PIECE LEFT...
...GUS'S PIECE!

AND THE CHICKENS STILL AREN'T IN THE MOOD TO SHARE! THEY TRIP GUS...
...MAKING HIM DROP HIS BREAKFAST...
WHICH AN OLD ROOSTER CLAIMS FOR HIMSELF.
TAKE IT EASY, CLUCK-CLUCK! LET IT GO!
WITH A SNORT, THE ROOSTER SHAKES HIS HEAD...
...UNTIL GUS LOSES HIS GRIP ON THAT LAST PIECE OF CORN.

OH!
GET OUT OF HERE! SHOO! SHOO!
POOR LITTLE GUS.
HERE.
HELP YOURSELF!

"HELP YOURSELF" MIGHT HAVE BEEN THE TWO MOST WONDERFUL WORDS GUS HAD EVER HEARD.
MEANWHILE, THE OTHER MICE ARE MAKING THEIR WAY BACK TO THE KITCHEN...
GULP!
BUT LUCIFER IS WATCHING THE ROOM CAREFULLY, STILL HUNTING FOR JAQ. IF HE SPOTS THEM, THEY'RE DONE FOR!

LUCKILY JAQ SPOTS THEM FIRST...
AND PROVIDES THE PERFECT DISTRACTION!

WITH LUCIFER FOCUSED ON WHERE HE THOUGHT HE SAW JAQ --
--THE OTHERS ARE FREE TO MAKE THEIR WAY BACK ACROSS THE KITCHEN.
BUT THEY'LL HAVE TO HURRY!
THE MICE RUN SO FAST, ONE OF THEM DROPS SOME OF HIS FOOD...

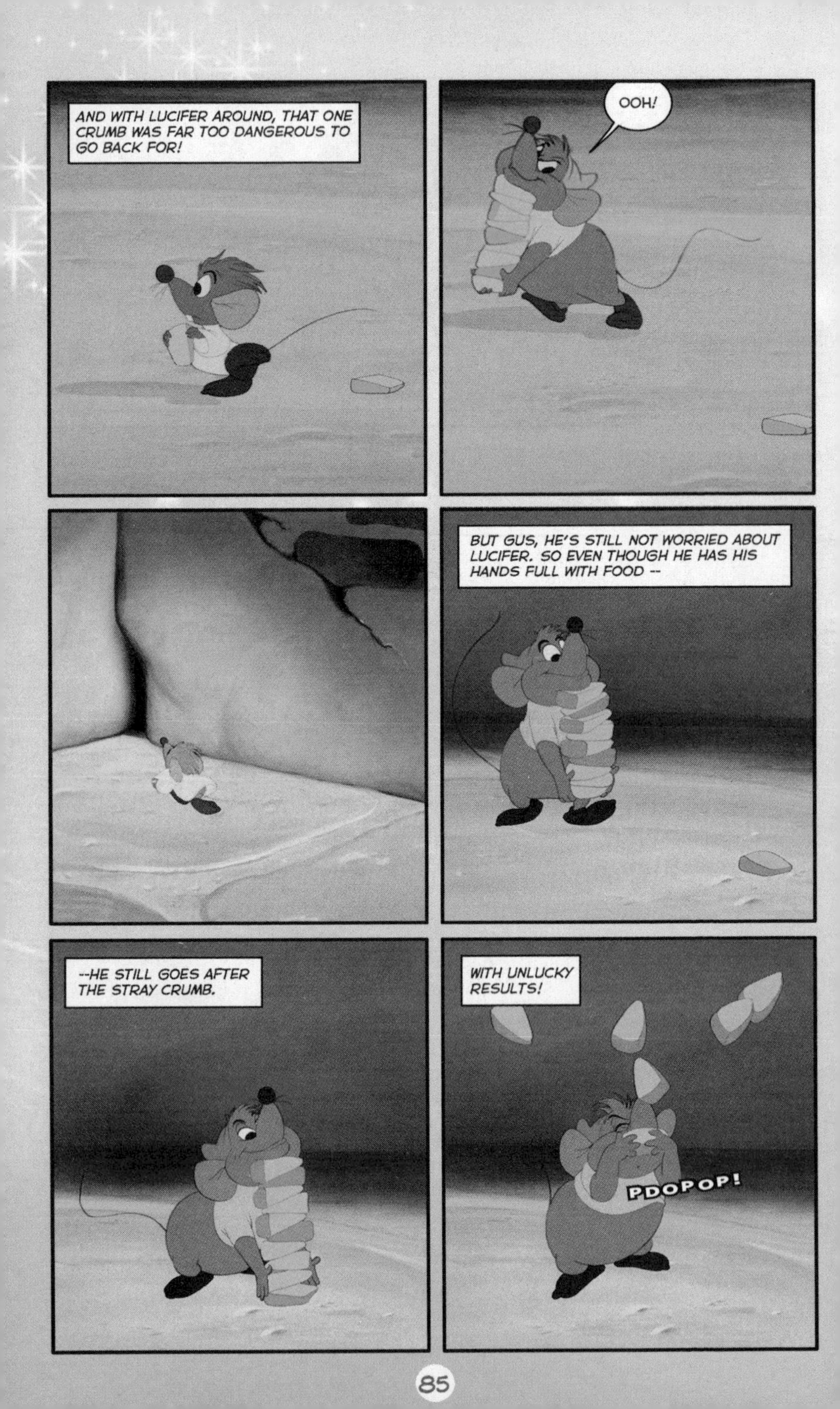
AND WITH LUCIFER AROUND, THAT ONE CRUMB WAS FAR TOO DANGEROUS TO GO BACK FOR!
OOH!
BUT GUS, HE'S STILL NOT WORRIED ABOUT LUCIFER. SO EVEN THOUGH HE HAS HIS HANDS FULL WITH FOOD --
--HE STILL GOES AFTER THE STRAY CRUMB.
WITH UNLUCKY RESULTS!
PDOPOP!

VERY UNLUCKY!
MRRROW?
LUCIFER'S KEEN EARS HEARD THE SOUND OF THE SPILLING FOOD.
GASP!
AND SUDDENLY...
LUCIFER FORGOT ALL ABOUT JAQ.
HIS ATTENTION WAS SQUARELY ON GUS.

A FATTER MOUSE.
A TASTIER MOUSE.
A MOUSE TOO BUSY PICKING UP CRUMBS TO SEE HIM COMING!
UGH!
POIT!
EVEN PULLING OUT ONE OF LUCIFER'S WHISKERS DIDN'T MAKE THE CAT LOOK AWAY!

JAQ KNOWS HE HAS TO DO SOMETHING!
HFFFF--
PODOPOPOP
MMMM...

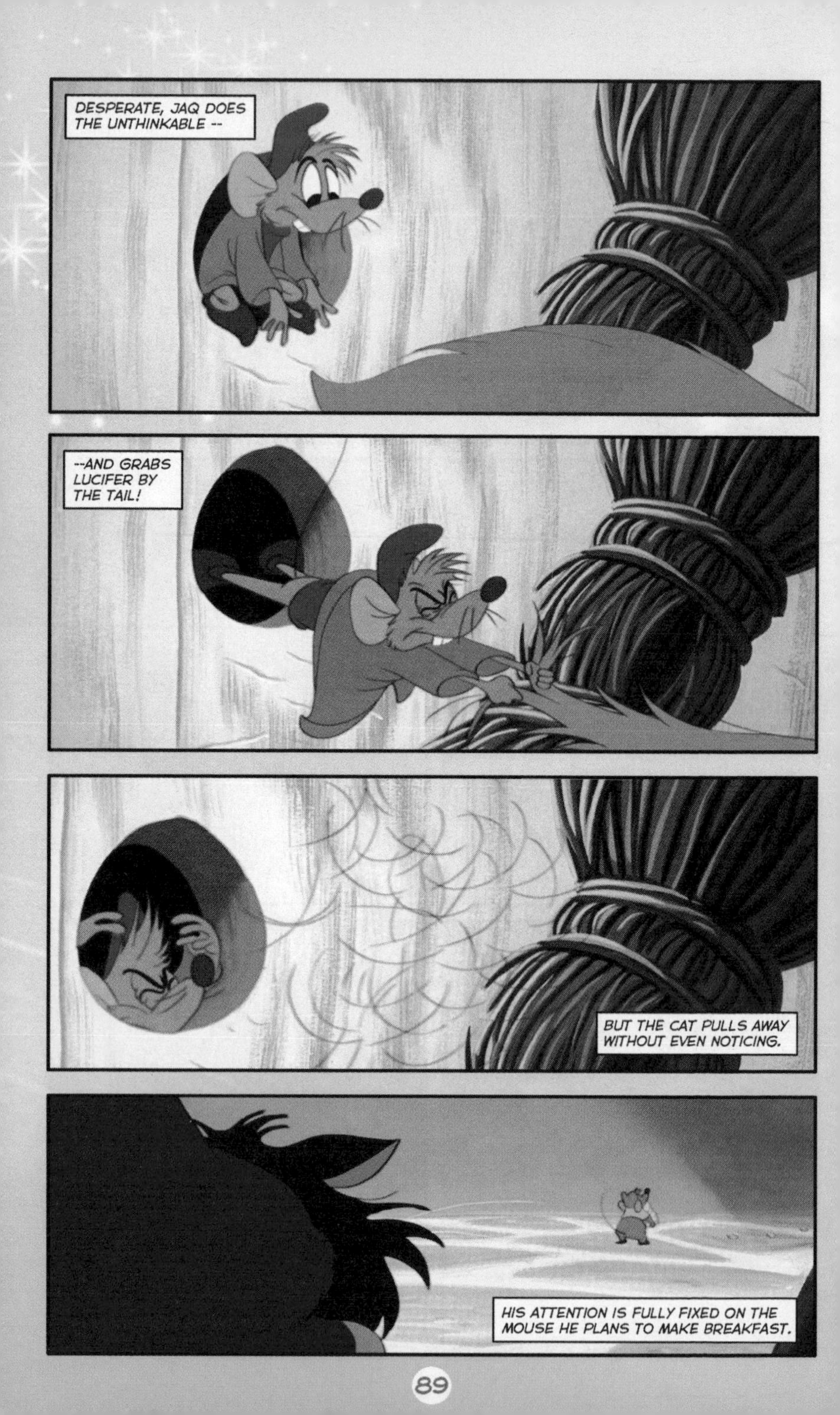
DESPERATE, JAQ DOES THE UNTHINKABLE --
--AND GRABS LUCIFER BY THE TAIL!
BUT THE CAT PULLS AWAY WITHOUT EVEN NOTICING.
HIS ATTENTION IS FULLY FIXED ON THE MOUSE HE PLANS TO MAKE BREAKFAST.

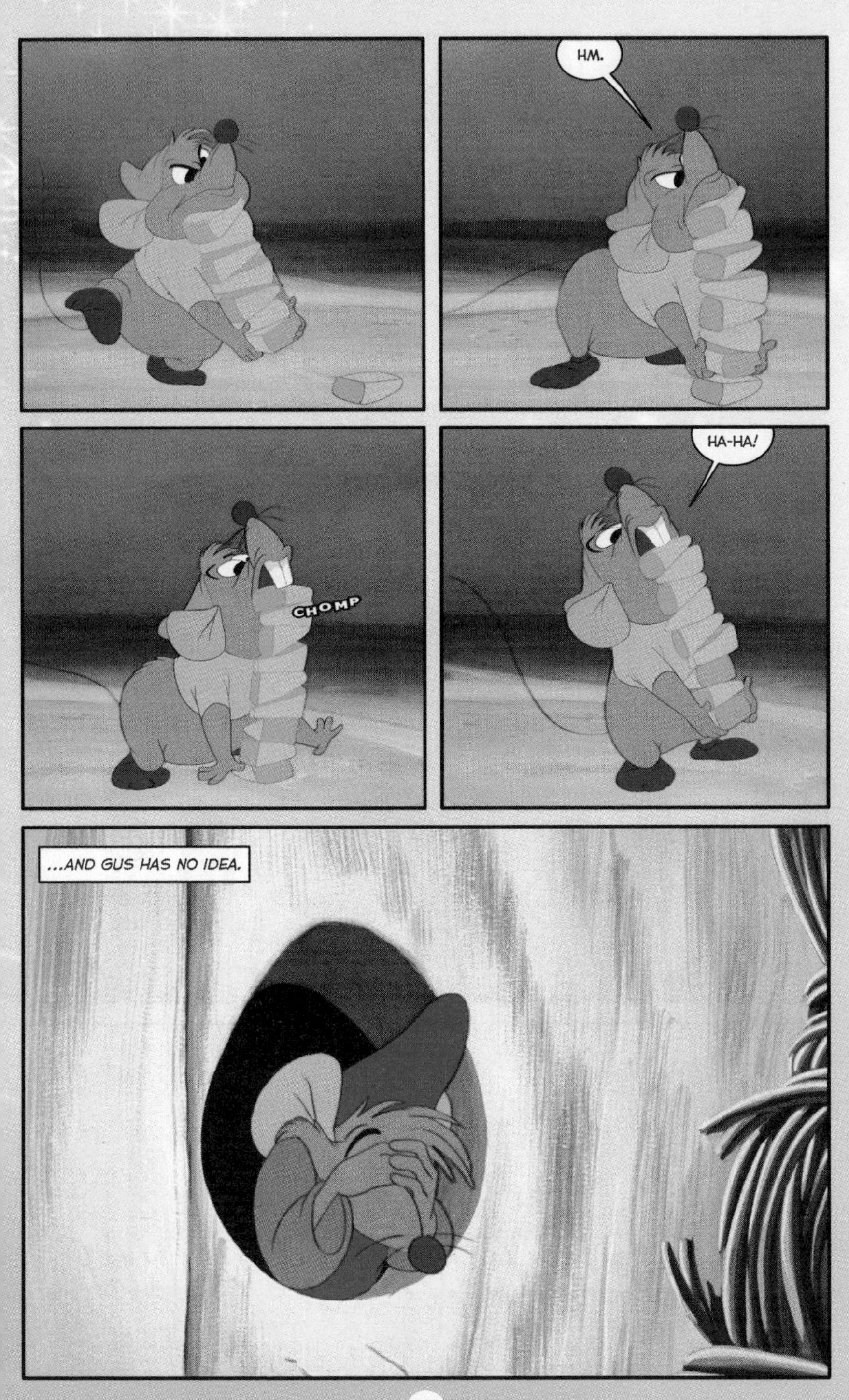
HM.
CHOMP
HA-HA!
...AND GUS HAS NO IDEA.

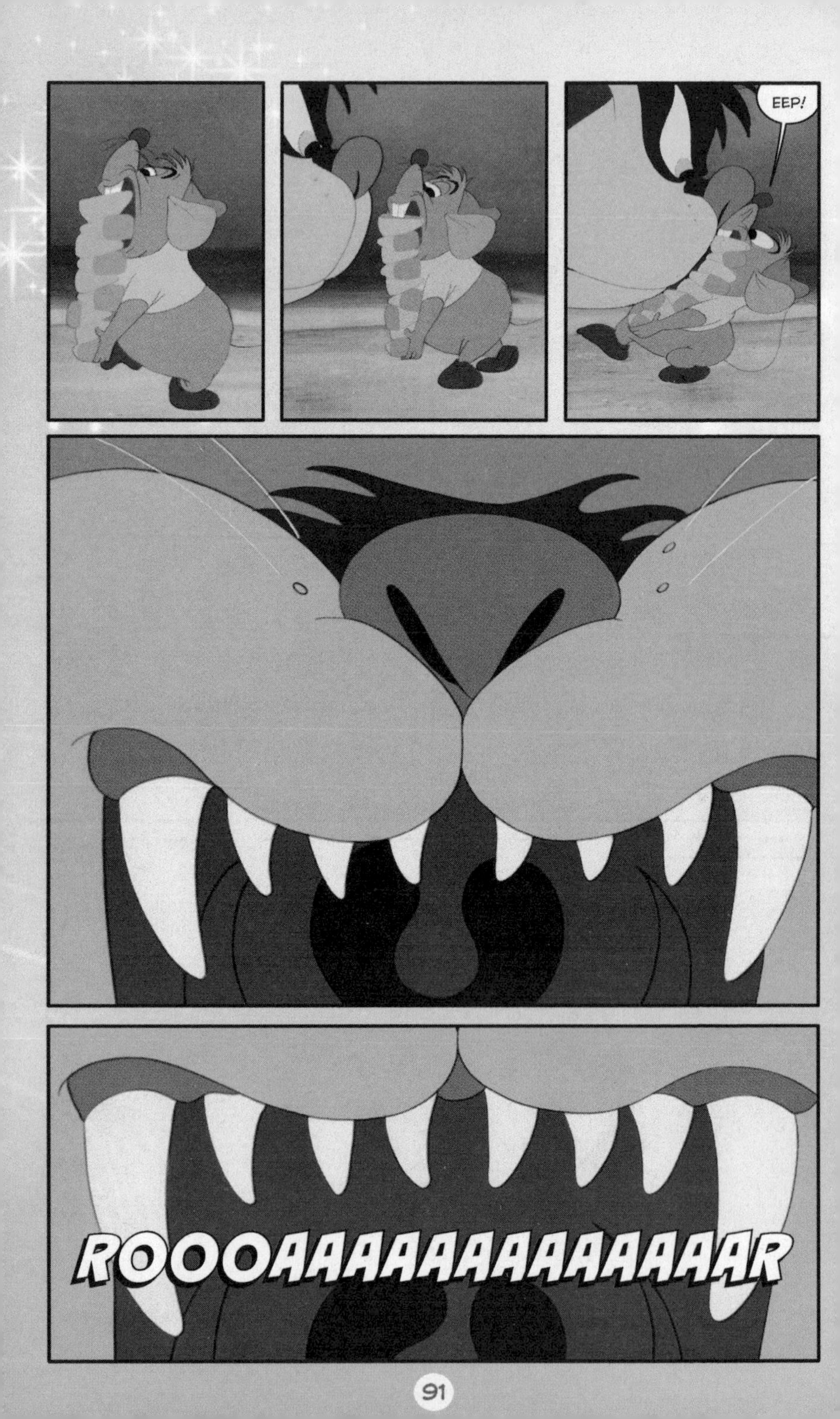
EEP!
ROOOAAAAAAAAAAAAAAR

DOH-OH!
NOW GUS REALIZES WHAT KIND OF TROUBLE HE'S IN, AND TRIES TO RUN --
--BUT HE'S NOT GETTING ANYWHERE.
LUCIFER HAS THE MOUSE RIGHT WHERE HE WANTS HIM.

BUT JAQ ISN'T ABOUT TO LET GUS GET EATEN.
HE LEANS OUT OF HIS HOLE IN THE WALL AND PUSHES A NEARBY BROOM FOR ALL HE'S WORTH!
HEH HEH HEH.
AND WHEN THE BROOM FINALLY TIPS OVER...
WHUNGGG
...IT KNOCKS LUCIFER SILLY!

MRRROW?
HUH. NO GUS-GUS.
GUESS HE GOT AWAY.
LUCIFER CAN'T BELIEVE IT. WHAT HAPPENED?
WHERE HAD HIS BREAKFAST RUN OFF TO?
LUCIFER LOOKED AROUND THE ROOM.

...FINALLY SPOTTING GUS, MAKING HIS WAY UP A TABLECLOTH.
PANT *PANT*
WHEW!

GUS IS SO WINDED FROM HIS ESCAPE --
DUH-HOH?
HE DOESN'T SEE LUCIFER COMING, AND GETS TRAPPED UNDER A TEACUP!
CLACK
AND, JUST WHEN IT LOOKS LIKE IT'S ALL OVER FOR POOR GUS...
ding ding
CINDERELLA!!

HE'S QUITE LITERALLY SAVED BY THE BELL...
...AS CINDERELLA'S STEPSISTERS CALL HER BACK INTO THE CHATEAU.
ALL RIGHT, ALL RIGHT, I'M COMING!
OH, MY GOODNESS.
FEH.
MORNING, NOON, AND NIGHT.

ding
ding
CINDERELLA!!
I'M COMING,
I'M COMING...
AN EVIL GRIN CREEPS
ACROSS LUCIFER'S FACE.
NOW THAT CINDERELLA
IS DISTRACTED...
...HE CAN GET BACK TO
HIS TRAPPED MOUSE.

BUT WHEN LUCIFER GETS BACK UP TO THE TABLE, HE FINDS THREE OVERTURNED TEACUPS!
WHICH ONE HID THE MOUSE?
WHICH ONE??

HEH!
LUCIFER THINKS HE HAS THE RIGHT CUP NOW. ALL HE NEEDS TO DO IS -
ding ding
I'M COMING! JUST A MINUTE...

LUCIFER IS DETERMINED TO GET HOLD OF GUS BEFORE CINDERELLA CAN STOP HIM.
HE JUST NEEDS TO FIND HIM!
AND LUCIFER IS IN SUCH A RUSH...
...HE ALMOST LOST HIS BREAKFAST AGAIN.

BUT NOW HE HAD IT. HE --
HE COULD HEAR CINDERELLA RETURNING.
ding ding ding ding ding
JUST A MINUTE...
ding ding ding ding ding
ding ding ding ding ding

ding ding ding
ding ding ding
CINDERELLA!!
CINDERELLA CONTINUES TO PREPARE BREAKFAST FOR HER STEPMOTHER AND STEPSISTERS, AS QUICKLY AS SHE CAN...
...WHILE LUCIFER WAITS FOR HER TO TURN HER ATTENTION AWAY FROM HIS MOUSE. HE DOESN'T WANT HER TO TAKE IT FROM HIM.
BUT SHE HAS!
AND LUCIFER REALIZES THAT THE MOUSE MUST STILL BE UNDER ONE OF THE TEACUPS!

AND LUCIFER IS GOING TO FIND OUT.
HE'S GOING TO FOLLOW AND WATCH...
THERE MAY BE A CHANCE YET TO CLAIM HIS PRIZE.
THE MOUSE IS STILL THERE!

LUCIFER SLINKS
UP THE STAIRS...

... AND WAITS FOR
HIS CHANCE.

ALL CINDERELLA HAS TO DO IS GET A LITTLE CLOSER AND...
AND THE MOUSE IS GONE AGAIN?
GOOD MORNING, DRIZELLA. SLEEP WELL?
FEH. AS IF YOU CARE.

LUCIFER IS CONFOUNDED. HOW DID HIS BREAKFAST ESCAPE AGAIN?
MAYBE THE MOUSE WOULD COME RUNNING OUT OF THE ROOM. LUCIFER COULD WAIT.
TAKE THAT IRONING AND HAVE IT BACK IN AN HOUR. ONE HOUR, DO YOU HEAR?
YES, DRIZELLA.
WAS THE MOUSE IN DRIZELLA'S ROOM?
BUMP
NOT THERE.

BUT THERE WERE STILL TEACUPS LEFT TO CHECK.
AND LUCIFER WAS COMMITTED. THAT MOUSE WOULD NOT INSULT HIM BY ESCAPING!
GOOD MORNING, ANASTASIA.
WELL, IT'S ABOUT TIME! DON'T FORGET THE MENDING!
DON'T BE ALL DAY GETTING IT DONE, EITHER!
YES, ANASTASIA.

AGAIN, LUCIFER LOOKED FOR HIS PREY.
WHUMP
AND AGAIN, HE TOOK A BUMP IN THE NOSE FROM A CLOSING DOOR.
AHEM.
GOOD MORNING, STEPMOTHER.
OH COME IN,CHILD, COME IN!
PICK UP THE LAUNDRY AND GET ON WITH YOUR DUTIES.
YES, STEPMOTHER.

LUCIFER SNEAKS FORWARD, CERTAIN THE MOUSE WAS CLOSE AT HAND.
BDUMP
MROW. FFFT.
THE MOUSE WAS DID NOT ESCAPE WITH THE LAUNDRY.

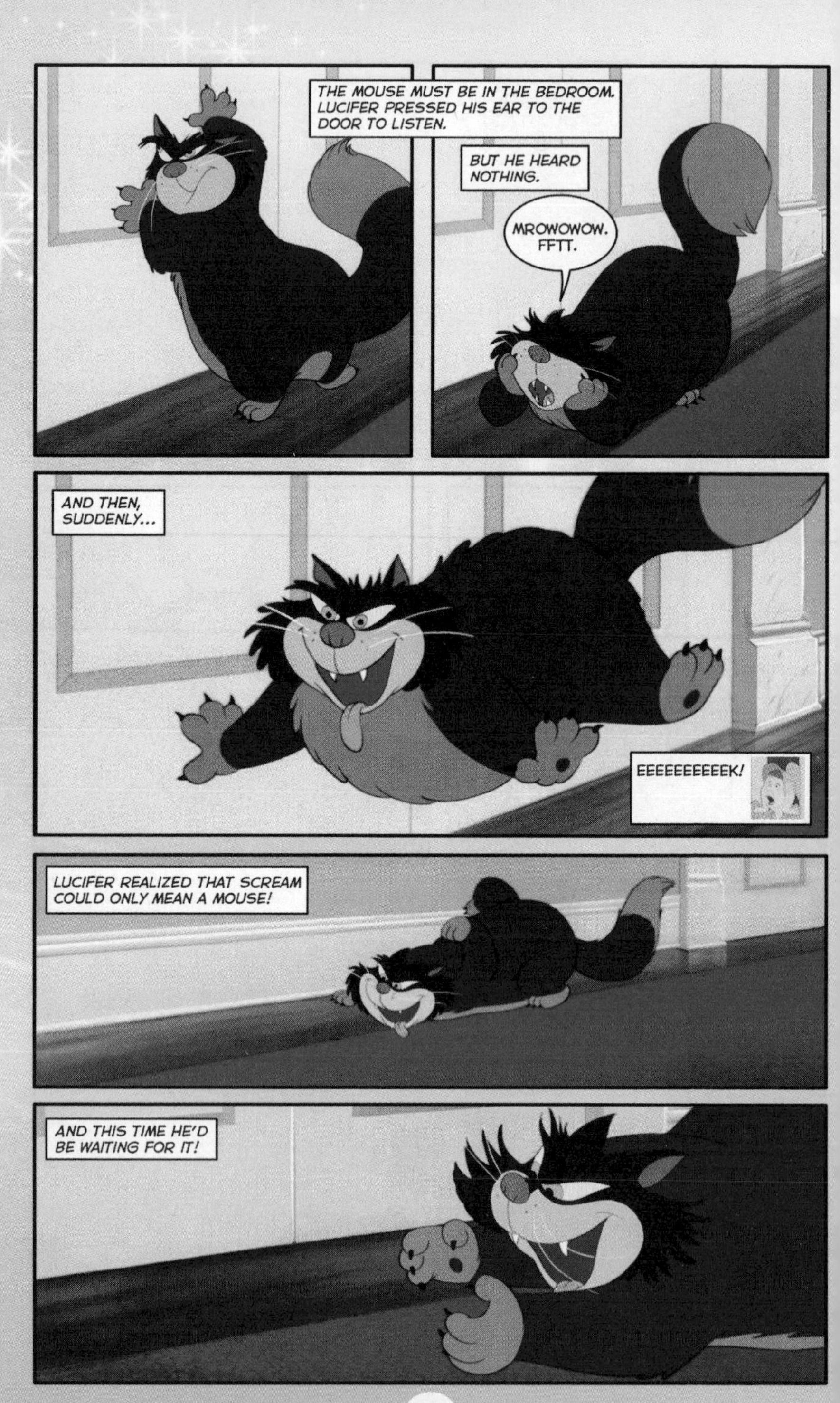
THE MOUSE MUST BE IN THE BEDROOM. LUCIFER PRESSED HIS EAR TO THE DOOR TO LISTEN.
BUT HE HEARD NOTHING.
MROWOWOW. FFTT.
AND THEN, SUDDENLY...
EEEEEEEEEEK!
LUCIFER REALIZED THAT SCREAM COULD ONLY MEAN A MOUSE!
AND THIS TIME HE'D BE WAITING FOR IT!

OOOOOH!
MOTHER!
OH, MOTHER! MOTHERRRR!
YOU DID IT!

YOU DID IT ON PURPOSE!
OH, MOTHER, MOTHER, MOTHER!
NOW WHAT DID YOU DO?
SHE PUT IT THERE!
A BIG UGLY MOUSE! RIGHT UNDER MY TEACUP!

ALL RIGHT, LUCIFER.
WHAT DID YOU DO WITH IT?
OH, YOU'RE NOT FOOLING ME. WE'LL JUST SEE ABOUT THIS.
COME ON. LET HIM GO.

NOW THE OTHER ONE. COME ON!
OH. POOR LITTLE GUS.
OH, LUCIFER. WON'T YOU EVER LEARN?

CINDERELLA!

YES, STEPMOTHER.
ARE YOU GONNA GET IT!

COME HERE.

PLEASE, YOU DON'T THINK THAT I --
HOLD YOUR TONGUE.
IT SEEMS WE HAVE TIME ON OUR HANDS.
BUT I WAS ONLY TRYING TO --
SILENCE.
TIME FOR VICIOUS PRACTICAL JOKES.

PERHAPS WE CAN PUT IT TO BETTER USE.
NOW, LET ME SEE...
THERE'S THE LARGE CARPET IN THE MAIN HALL... CLEAN IT.
AND THE WINDOWS, UPSTAIRS AND DOWN. WASH THEM.
AND THE TAPESTRIES. AND THE DRAPERIES.
BUT I JUST FINISHED --

DO THEM AGAIN.
DON'T FORGET THE GARDEN. THEN SCRUB THE TERRACE. SWEEP THE HALLS, AND THE STAIRS.
CLEAN THE CHIMNEYS.
AND OF COURSE, THERE'S THE MENDING. AND THE SEWING. AND THE LAUNDRY.
OH YES, AND ONE MORE THING --
--SEE THAT LUCIFER GETS HIS BATH.

LUCIFER SCOWLS AS IF TO ASK 'WHY SHOULD I BE PUNISHED, TOO?'
MEANWHILE, NOT FAR AWAY, AT THE ROYAL PALACE...
KNASH

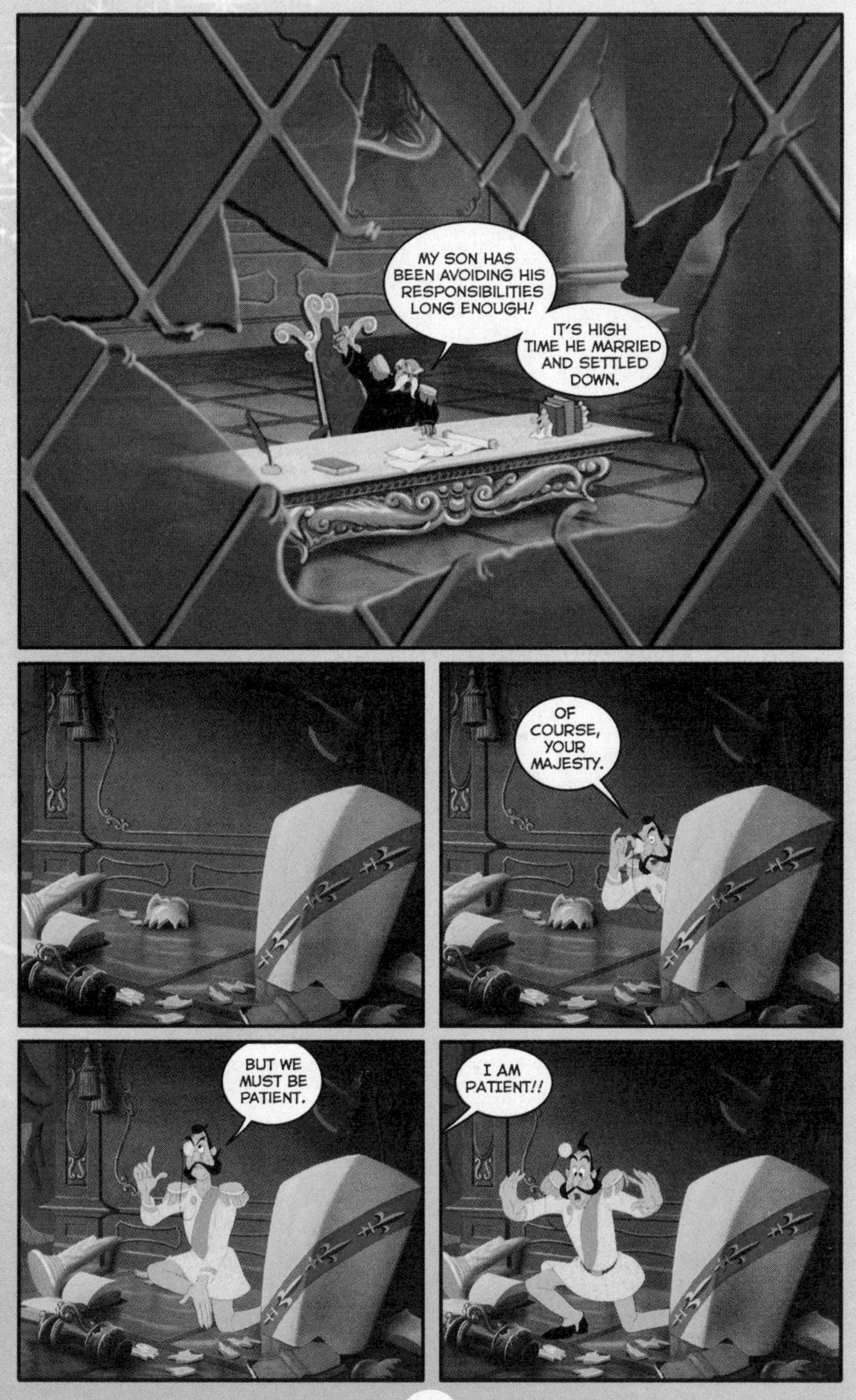
MY SON HAS BEEN AVOIDING HIS RESPONSIBILITIES LONG ENOUGH!
IT'S HIGH TIME HE MARRIED AND SETTLED DOWN.
OF COURSE, YOUR MAJESTY.
BUT WE MUST BE PATIENT.
I AM PATIENT!!

OH!
KRSPLASH
I'M NOT GETTING ANY YOUNGER, YOU KNOW.
I WANT TO SEE MY GRANDCHILDREN BEFORE I GO.
I UNDERSTAND, SIRE.
NO.

NO, YOU DON'T KNOW WHAT IT MEANS...
...TO SEE YOUR ONLY CHILD...
...GROW FARTHER...
...FARTHER...
...AND FARTHER AWAY FROM YOU.
I'M LONELY IN THIS DESOLATE OLD PALACE.

I WANT TO HEAR THE PITTER-PATTER OF LITTLE FEET AGAIN.

NOW NOW, YOUR MAJESTY.
SOB!

HONK

PERHAPS IF WE JUST LET HIM ALONE...

LET HIM ALONE?!?

WITH HIS --
-- HIS SILLY ROMANTIC IDEAS?!?
BUT... BUT SIRE...
IN MATTERS OF LOVE --
"LOVE." BAH.

JUST A BOY MEETING A GIRL UNDER THE RIGHT CONDITIONS.
PLATO
SO WE'RE ARRANGING THE CONDITIONS.
BUT YOUR MAJESTY - IF THE PRINCE SHOULD SUSPECT...

SUSPECT. HAH!
LOOK, THE BOY'S COMING HOME TODAY, ISN'T HE?
YES, SIRE.
WELL, WHAT COULD BE MORE NATURAL...
...THAN A BALL TO CELEBRATE HIS RETURN?
N-NOTHING, SIRE!
AND IF ALL THE ELIGIBLE MAIDENS IN MY KINGDOM JUST HAPPENED TO BE THERE...

HEH HEH.
HE'S BOUND TO SHOW INTEREST IN ONE OF THEM, ISN'T HE?
ISN'T HE?!?
Y-Y-Y-YES, SIRE?
THE MOMENT HE DOES... SOFT LIGHTS, ROMANTIC MUSIC?
ALL THE TRIMMINGS! HA HA.

IT CAN'T POSSIBLY FAIL, CAN IT?
YES SIRE. ER - N-NO, SIRE. AH, VERY WELL, SIRE.
I WILL ARRANGE THE BALL FOR --
TONIGHT.
TONIGHT? OH, BUT SIRE --

TONIGHT.
AND SEE THAT EVERY ELIGIBLE MAID IS THERE.
UNDERSTAND?
SIGH.
YES, YOUR MAJESTY.

AND, BACK AT THE CHATEAU... CINDERELLA'S STEPSISTERS CONTINUE THEIR MUSIC LESSONS...
THE PEAR SHAPED TONES...
FEH!
...MUCH TO LUCIFER'S CHAGRIN.
LA LA LA LA LAAAAA
THEY'VE PRACTICED FOR MOST OF THEIR LIVES. BUT DRIZELLA'S SHRILL VOICE AND ANASTASIA'S OFF-KEY FLUTE PLAYING...
...WELL, THEY HAVEN'T SHOWN MUCH IMPROVEMENT.

OH-OH-OH
-OH-OHHHH
ERK!
...AND LUCIFER'S KEEN EARS
CAN ONLY TAKE SO MUCH.
BUT THEN, HE HEARS
SOMETHING ELSE.
CINDERELLA, SINGING TO
HERSELF AS SHE WORKS.
CINDERELLA'S VOICE
IS BEAUTIFUL.
SO ENCHANTING, IT
ALMOST CAPTURES
LUCIFER'S ATTENTION.
ALMOST.

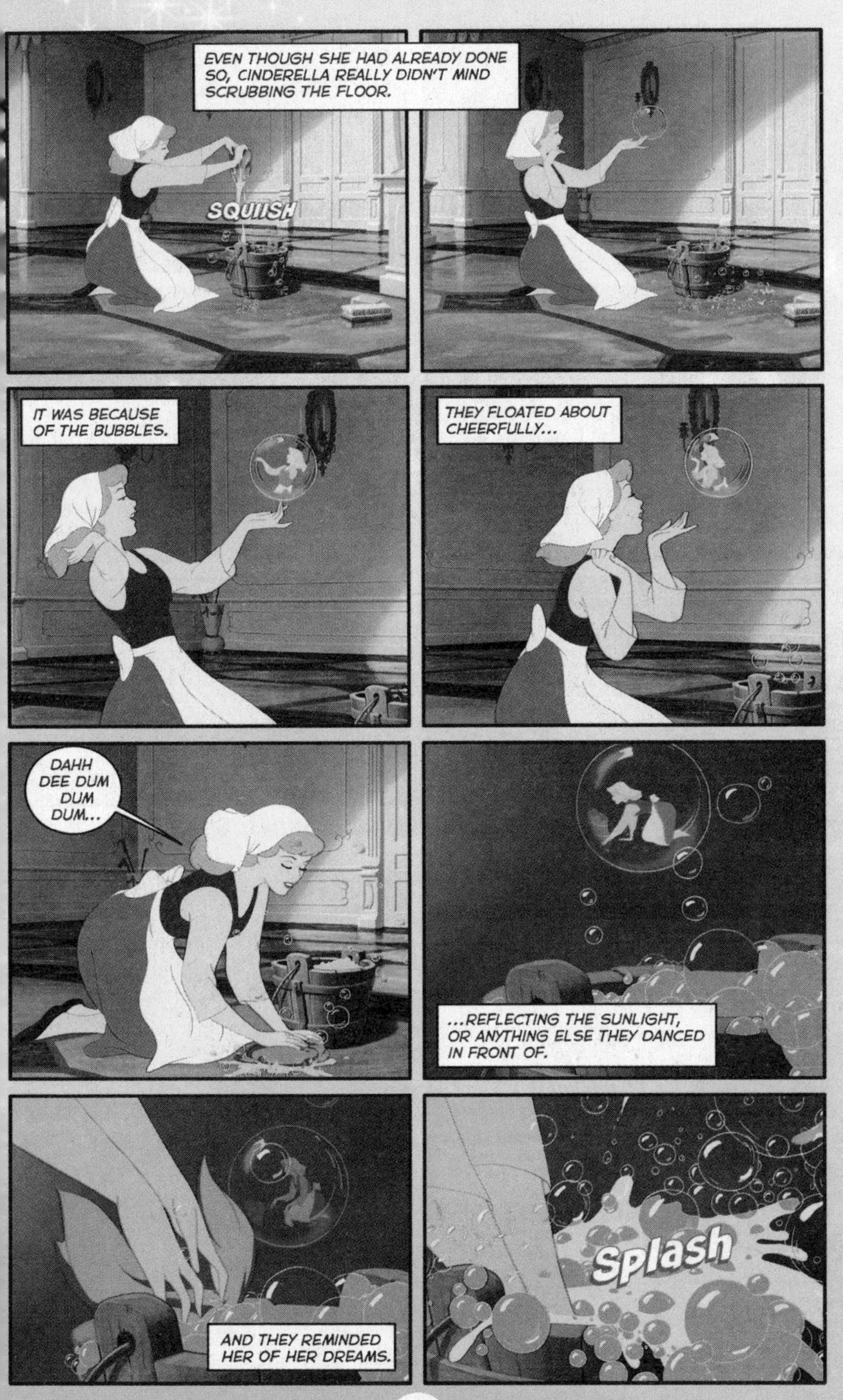

EVEN THOUGH SHE HAD ALREADY DONE SO, CINDERELLA REALLY DIDN'T MIND SCRUBBING THE FLOOR.
SQUIISH
IT WAS BECAUSE OF THE BUBBLES.
THEY FLOATED ABOUT CHEERFULLY...
DAHH DEE DUM DUM DUM...
...REFLECTING THE SUNLIGHT, OR ANYTHING ELSE THEY DANCED IN FRONT OF.
AND THEY REMINDED HER OF HER DREAMS.
Splash

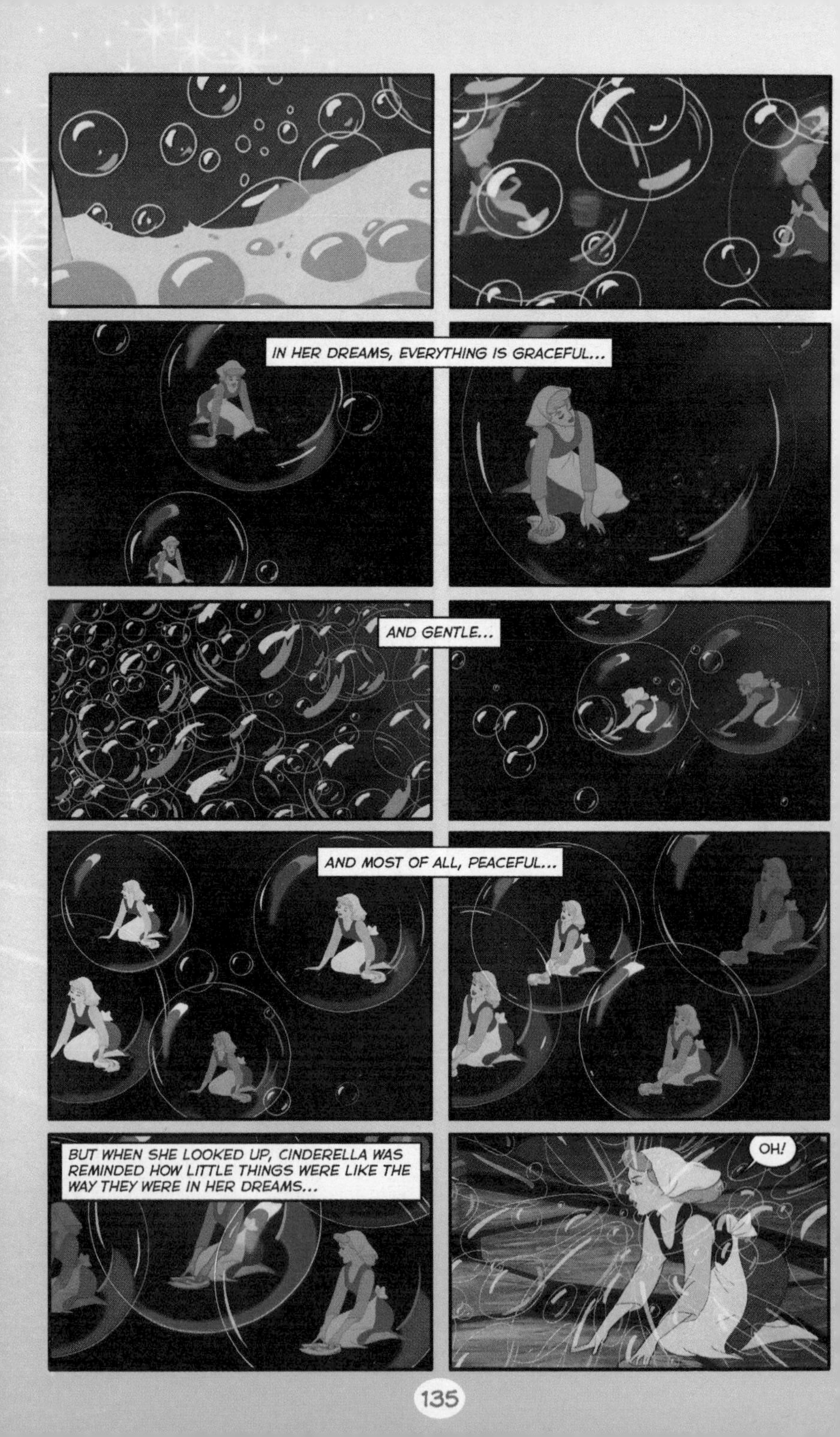
IN HER DREAMS, EVERYTHING IS GRACEFUL...
AND GENTLE...
AND MOST OF ALL, PEACEFUL...
BUT WHEN SHE LOOKED UP, CINDERELLA WAS REMINDED HOW LITTLE THINGS WERE LIKE THE WAY THEY WERE IN HER DREAMS...
OH!

OH, LUCIFER!
WHILE CINDERELLA HAD BEEN SINGING, LUCIFER HAD DECIDED TO PLAY - AND LEAVE A TRAIL OF DUST ALL ACROSS THE FRESHLY-SCRUBBED FLOOR.
YOU MEAN OLD THING!
I'M JUST GOING TO HAVE TO TEACH YOU A LESSON!

KNOCK
KNOCK
KNOCK
OPEN IN THE NAME OF THE KING!
AN URGENT MESSAGE FROM HIS IMPERIAL MAJESTY.
THANK YOU.

STILL GIGGLING, AND WORRIED LUCIFER MAY STILL BE HANGING ABOUT, JAQ AND GUS RETURN TO THE CHATEAU WALLS.

DRIZELLA AND ANASTASIA CONTINUE TO, WELL, TRY TO BE MUSICAL.
OH, SING SWEET NIGHTINGALE...
TOOOT
TOODOOOT
??
FAAA-FAAA-DII-DAAAAAAA!
TOOOT

TOOOT
YOU CLUMSY--!
BONK
YOU DID IT ON PURPOSE!
YOU'RE ALWAYS... UGH...IT'S HER FAULT, MOTHER!

GIRLS, GIRLS. ABOVE ALL, SELF-CONTROL.
KNOCK KNOCK
CINDERELLA!
I'VE WARNED YOU NEVER TO INTERRUPT WHILE --

BUT THIS JUST ARRIVED FROM THE PALACE!
FROM THE PALACE?!?
GIVE IT HERE!
LET ME HAVE IT!
I'LL READ IT.

WELL!
THERE'S TO BE A BALL.
A BALL!
IN HONOR OF HIS HIGHNESS, THE PRINCE!
AND BY ROYAL COMMAND, EVERY ELIGIBLE MAIDEN IS TO ATTEND!
OH, THE PRINCE!

WHY, THAT'S US!
AND I'M SO ELIGIBLE!
JAQ AND GUS HAVE TO BITE THEIR TONGUES SO AS TO NOT GIVE T HEMSELVES AWAY WITH LAUGHTER.
WHY, THAT MEANS I CAN GO, TOO!
HAH! HER DANCING WITH THE PRINCE!

"I'D BE HONORED, YOUR HIGHNESS..."

"...WOULD YOU MIND HOLDING MY BROOM?"
HAHA HA!

WELL, WHY NOT?

AFTER ALL, I'M STILL A MEMBER OF THE FAMILY.
AND IT SAYS'... BY ROYAL COMMAND...
...EVERY ELIGIBLE MAIDEN IS TO ATTEND.'
YES... SO IT DOES.
WELL, I SEE NO REASON WHY YOU CAN'T GO... IF YOU GET ALL YOUR WORK DONE.

OH,
I WILL!

I
PROMISE!

AND IF
YOU CAN FIND
SOMETHING
SUITABLE TO
WEAR...

I'M SURE
I CAN...

OH, THANK YOU,
STEPMOTHER!

MOTHER!
DO YOU REALIZE WHAT YOU JUST SAID?!?
OF COURSE.
...I SAID 'IF.'
OHHH.

'...IF.'
HEE HEE!
HAHAHA!
WHILE HER STEPMOTHER SMILES AT THE CRUEL JOKE, CINDERELLA LOOKS...
...FOR SOMETHING SPECIAL.
ISN'T IT LOVELY?

IT WAS MY MOTHER'S.
IT'S PRETTY-PRETTY, BUT IT'S OLD.
WELL, MAYBE IT IS A LITTLE OLD-FASHIONED...
...BUT I'LL FIX THAT.
DUH, BUT... BUT HOW YOU DO THAT, HUH?

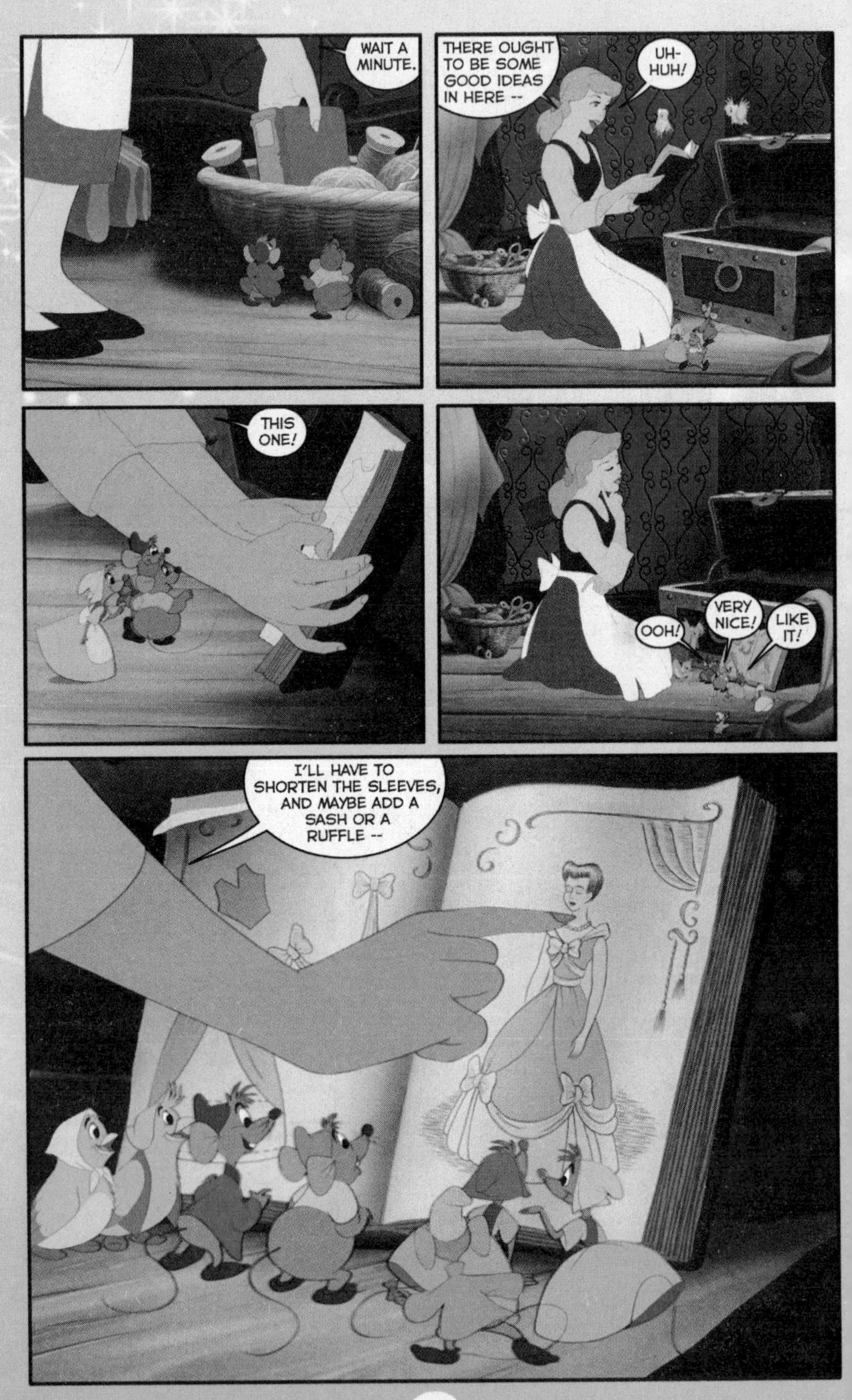
WAIT A MINUTE.
THERE OUGHT TO BE SOME GOOD IDEAS IN HERE --
UH-HUH!
THIS ONE!
OOH!
VERY NICE!
LIKE IT!
I'LL HAVE TO SHORTEN THE SLEEVES, AND MAYBE ADD A SASH OR A RUFFLE --

-- OR SOMETHING FOR THE COLLAR --
CINDERELLA!
OH NOW WHAT DO THEY WANT?
CINDERELLA!
CINDERELLA!
OH WELL. GUESS MY DRESS WILL JUST HAVE TO WAIT.
CINDERELLA!
ALL RIGHT, ALL RIGHT, I'M COMING...

POOR CINDERELLY.
THEY NEVER LEAVE HER ALONE!
ALWAYS CALLING AFTER HER.
"DO THIS!"
"DO THAT!"
CINDERELLA!
HMPH!

HMPH.
JACK KICKS AS HARD AS HE CAN TO SHUT THE DOOR...
...AND QUIET THE SHRILL VOICES OF CINDERELLA'S STEPSISTERS.
VOICES HE HEARS ALL TOO OFTEN.
SIGH
THEY NEVER QUIT!

ALL THE TIME -- ALWAYS YELLING!
"WHERE ARE YOU?!"
"COME HERE NOW!"
"NO, I NEED YOU MORE!"
"WHERE'S MY FOOD?!"
WE HEAR THEM, TOO!
ALWAYS AFTER HER!
ALWAYS SHOUTING!
THEY NEVER LET HER REST!

IT'S TRUE!
THEY KEEP HER SO BUSY --
SHE CAN BARELY SEE STRAIGHT!
AND THEN ALL SHE GETS --
EEP
--IN RETURN IS MORE CHORES TO DO.
SHE DOES EVERYTHING THEY ASK, AND THEY'RE NEVER HAPPY.
THEY JUST TELL HER TO GET BACK TO WORK...
POOR CINDERELLY.

YEAH, THEY KEEP HER BUSY.
TUMP
YOU KNOW WHAT?
CINDERELLY'S NOT GONNA GO TO THE BALL.

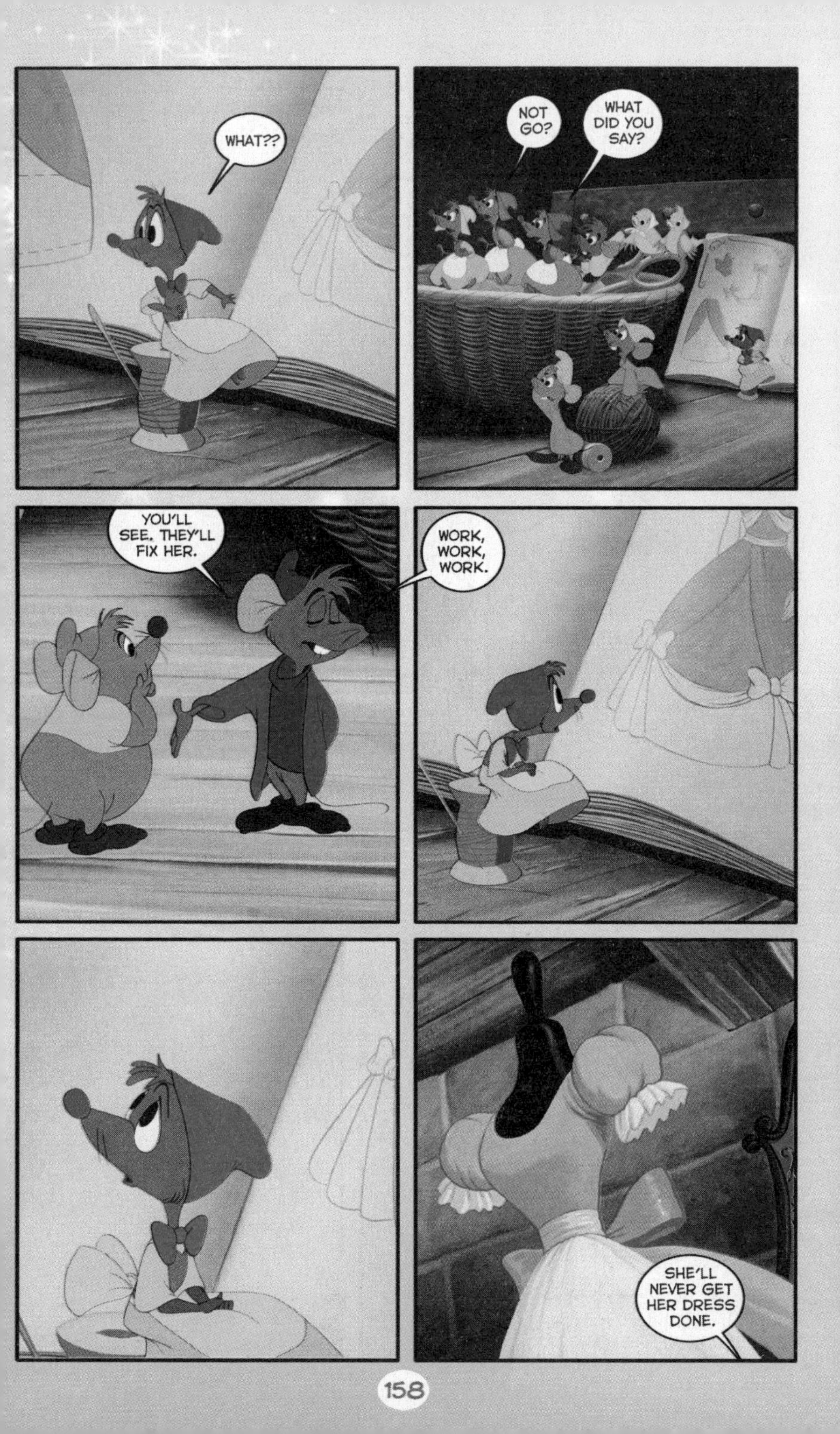
WHAT??
NOT GO?
WHAT DID YOU SAY?
YOU'LL SEE. THEY'LL FIX HER.
WORK, WORK, WORK.
SHE'LL NEVER GET HER DRESS DONE.

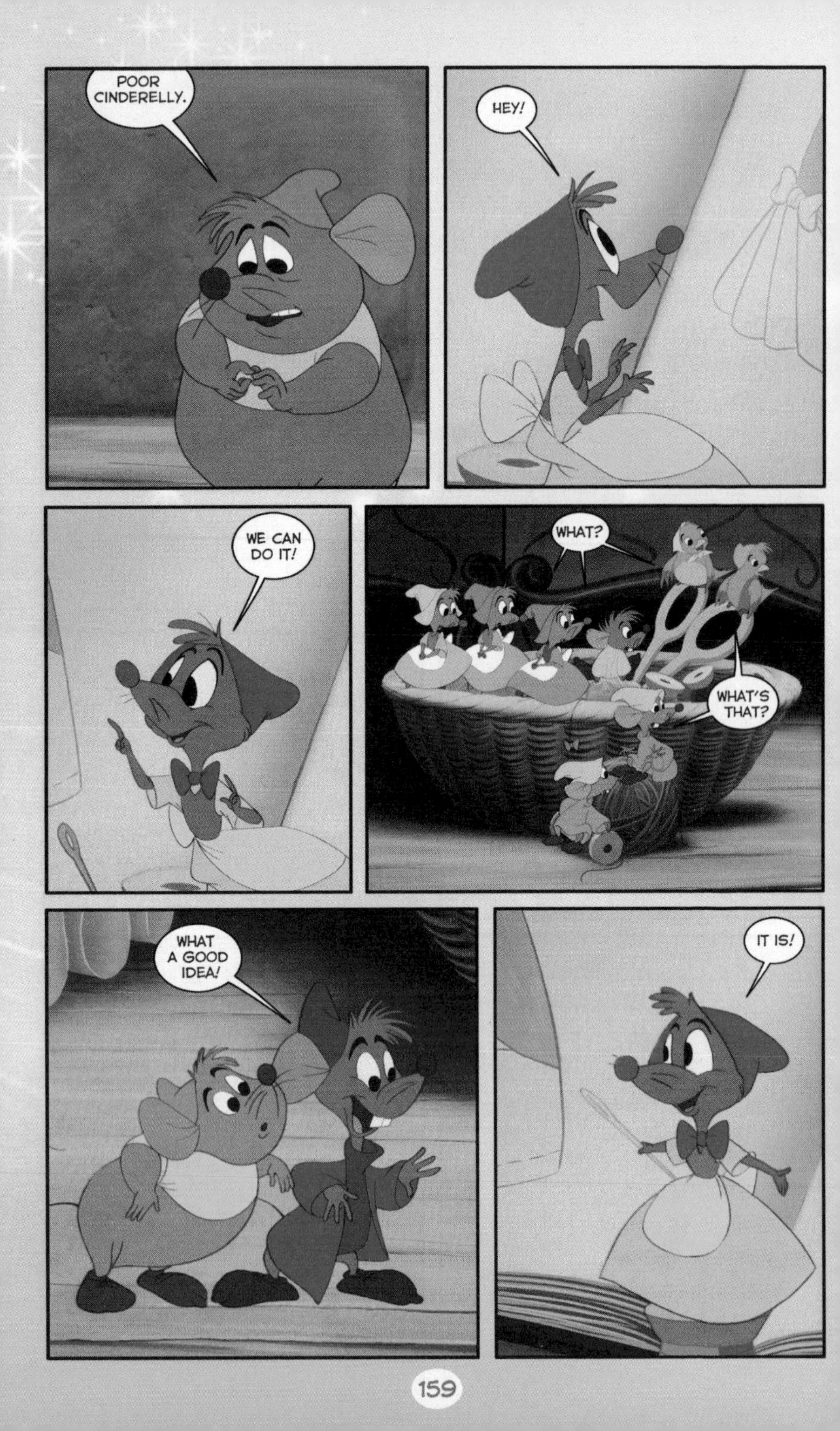
POOR CINDERELLY.
HEY!
WE CAN DO IT!
WHAT?
WHAT'S THAT?
WHAT A GOOD IDEA!
IT IS!

WE CAN DO IT!
WE CAN HELP HER GET IT DONE!
THERE'S NOTHING TO IT! WE HAVE EVERYTHING WE NEED!
SHE'LL GET TO DANCE AT THE BALL!
AND SHE'LL BE THE PRETTIEST ONE THERE!
WE'LL HELP!
YES - WE CAN GET SOME RIBBON!
I'LL CUT IT WITH THE SCISSORS!
AND I'LL --
YOU CAN GO LOOK FOR SOME TRIMMING!

OKAY, I WILL!
DUH, WAIT!
I'LL COME HELP, TOO!
FOLLOW ME, GUS-GUS!
I KNOW WHERE TO GO!
WE'LL FIND A PRETTY-PRETTY!
CINDERELLY WILL BE SURPRISED!
SURPRISE, SURPRISE! PRETTY SURPRISE FOR CINDERELLY!
JAQ AND GUS MAKE THEIR WAY THROUGH THE WALLS OF THE CHATEAU...
UNTIL THEY FIND THEIR SECRET WAY OUT.

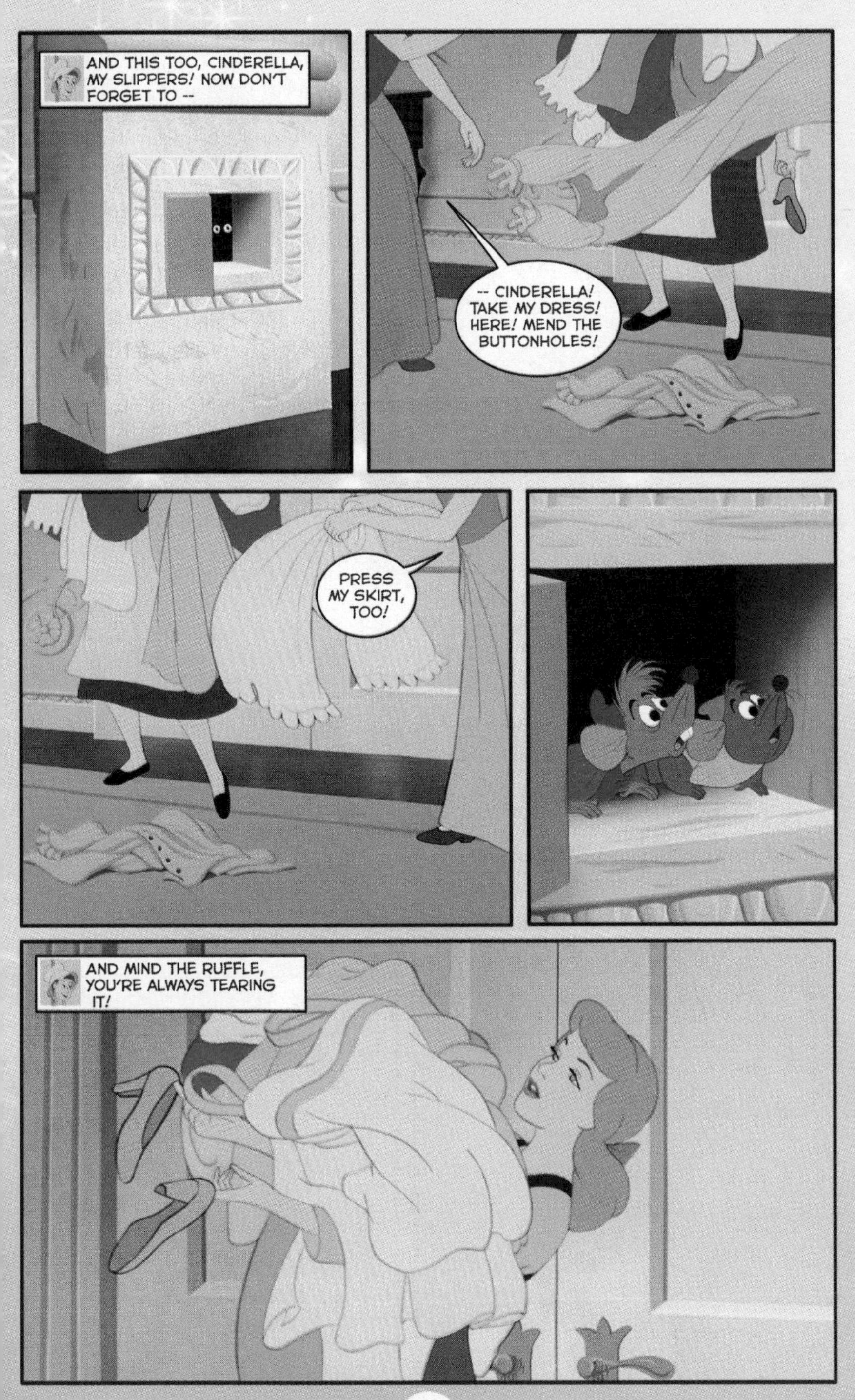

AND THIS TOO, CINDERELLA, MY SLIPPERS! NOW DON'T FORGET TO --
-- CINDERELLA! TAKE MY DRESS! HERE! MEND THE BUTTONHOLES!
PRESS MY SKIRT, TOO!
AND MIND THE RUFFLE, YOU'RE ALWAYS TEARING IT!

AND CINDERELLA--
YES?
WHEN YOU'RE THROUGH -
-- AND BEFORE YOU BEGIN YOUR REGULAR CHORES...
I HAVE A FEW LITTLE THINGS.
VERY WELL.

MOTHER, I DON'T SEE WHY EVERYBODY ELSE SEEMS TO HAVE SUCH NICE THINGS TO WEAR --
AND I ALWAYS END UP IN THESE OLD RAGS!
THIS SASH! WHY, I WOULDN'T BE SEEN DEAD IN IT!
YOU SHOULD TALK --

THESE BEADS! I'M SICK OF LOOKING AT THEM! TRASH!
JAQ AND GUS LIGHT UP AS ANASTASIA AND DRIZELLA CONTINUE TO COMPLAIN...
THAT SASH AND THOSE BEADS ARE JUST WHAT CINDERELLA'S DRESS NEEDS!
THEY JUST HAVE TO WAIT FOR THE SISTERS TO LEAVE...
COME ON!

NOW, BE CAREFEE...
YES, YES, YES. REAL CAREFEE.
THE MICE SNEAK PAST THE SLEEPING LUCIFER...
AND TOWARDS THE DISCARDED TRIMMINGS.
HO HO HO! WE CAN USE THAT, GUS-GUS!

YUP YUP! PRETTY PRETTY PRETTY PRETTY PRETTY!
SHH! LOOKIT!
LUCIFEE.
GUS IMMEDIATELY QUIETS HIMSELF AND HELPS JAQ QUIETLY RACE OFF WITH THE SASH.
MRRW?
JUST NOT QUITE QUIET ENOUGH.

RUSTLING AGAINST THE CARPET WOKE LUCIFER.
AND DREW HIS CURIOSITY.
WHAT HE SAW LOOKED LIKE A SASH UNROLLING BY ITSELF!
THIS MADE HIM EVEN MORE CURIOUS.
WHAT COULD BE DOING THIS? WAS IT MAGIC?

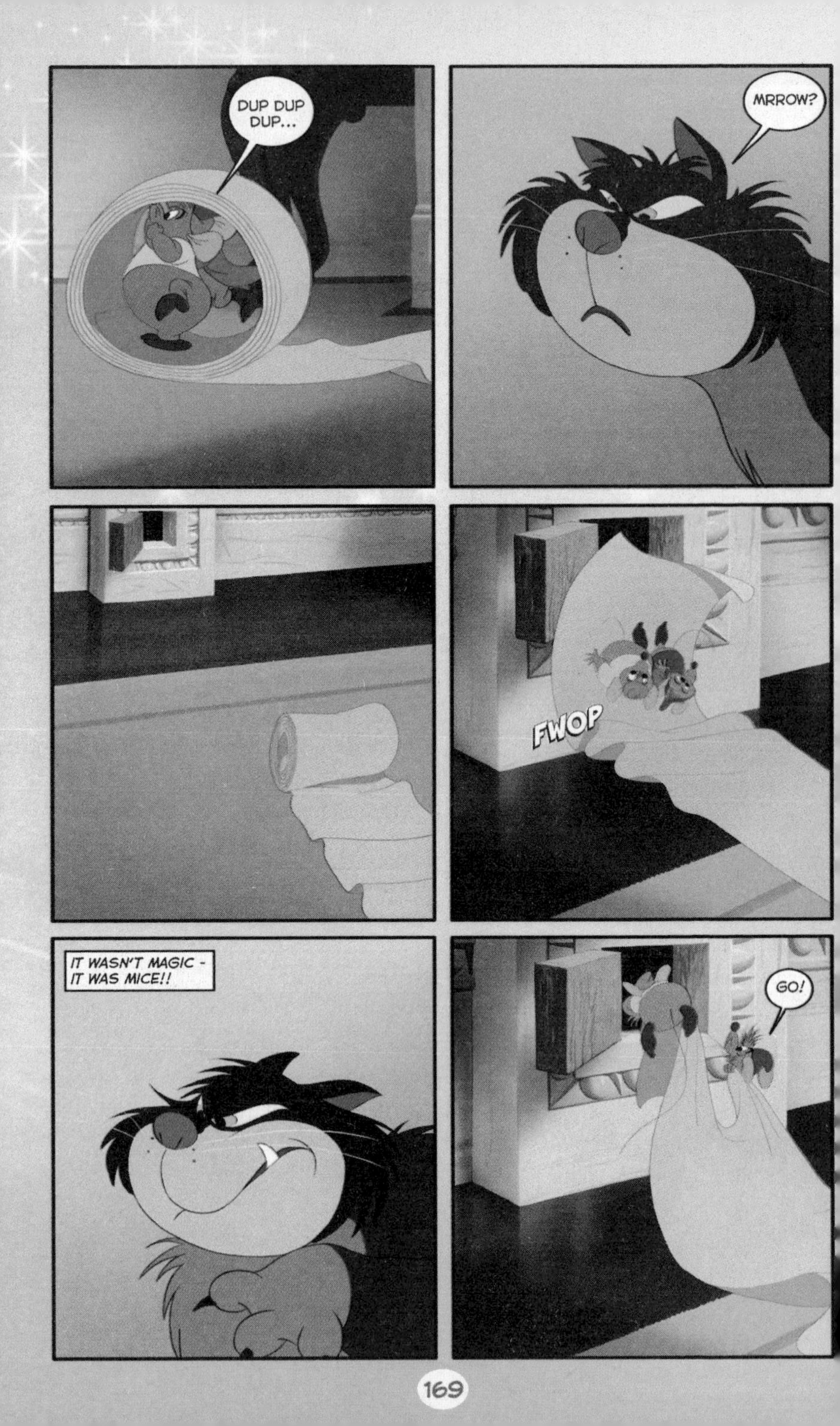
DUP DUP DUP...
MRROW?
FWOP
IT WASN'T MAGIC - IT WAS MICE!!
GO!

LUCIFER RACED FOR THE END OF THE SASH...
HOPING ONE GOOD TUG WOULD PULL THE MICE RIGHT OUT OF THE WALLS...
BOMP
BUT HE WASN'T FAST ENOUGH.
AND WHERE THEY WENT, HE COULD NOT FOLLOW.
MRROW!

POP!
BUT LUCIFER ISN'T GOING TO GIVE UP. MAYBE THE MICE WILL COME BACK --
CREEEEEEEEAAAAK
?
CREEEEEEEEAAAAK
DUH DUH.. WHAT?

OH, BEADS!! HOHOHO. VERY PRETTY BEADS!
SHHHH!
BUT IT WAS TOO LATE - LUCIFER HAD HEARD WHAT THEY WERE AFTER...
AND HE WOULD MAKE SURE THEY COULDN'T GET TO IT.

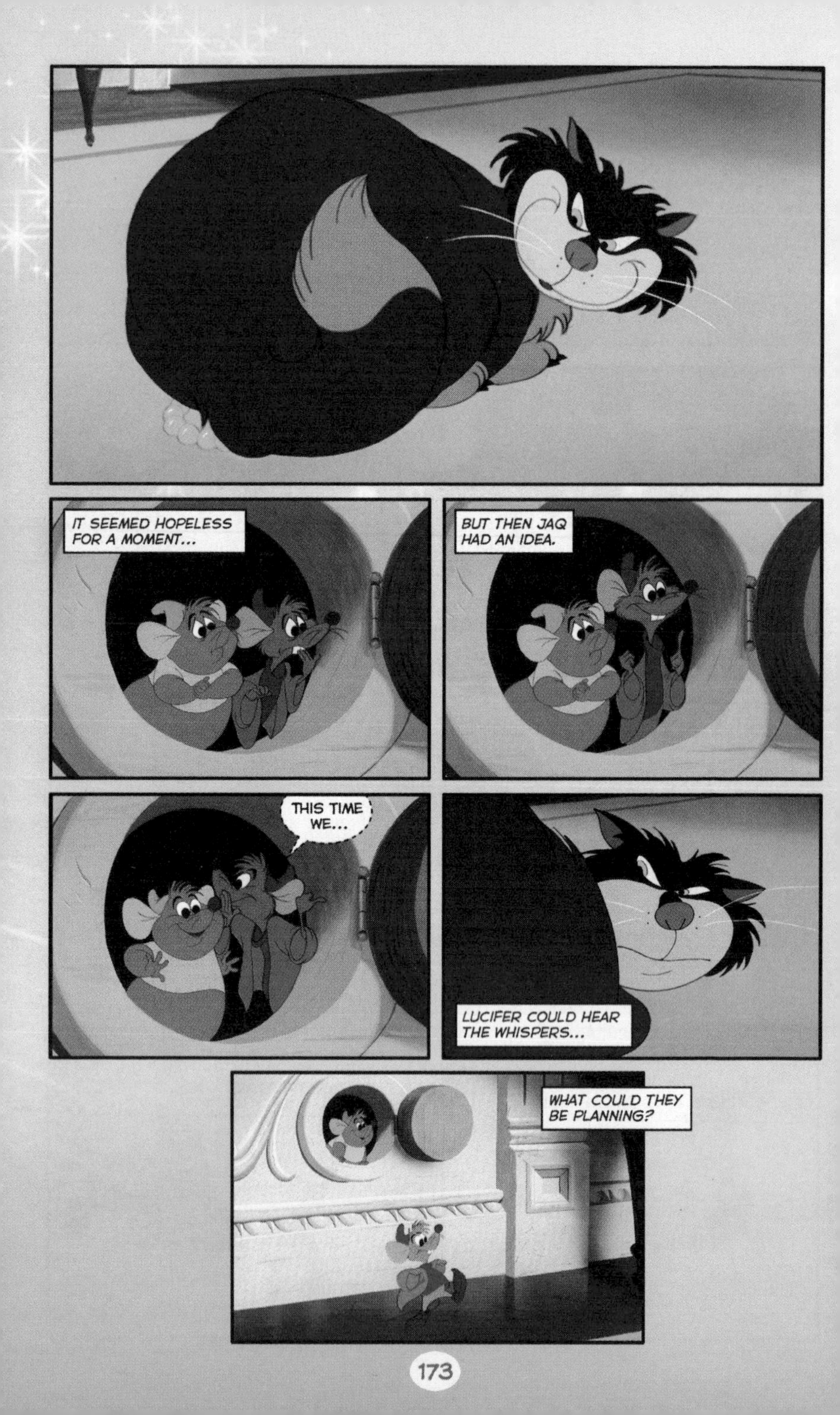
IT SEEMED HOPELESS FOR A MOMENT...
BUT THEN JAQ HAD AN IDEA.
THIS TIME WE...
LUCIFER COULD HEAR THE WHISPERS...
WHAT COULD THEY BE PLANNING?

IT DIDN'T MATTER. HE WAS READY FOR ANYTHING THIS TIME.
DEE DUM DE DUM...
BUM BUM BUM
EXCEPT, MAYBE, FOR THE MOUSE TO SNEAK PAST HIM WHILE HUMMING A TUNE!
AS FAR AS LUCIFER WAS CONCERNED, IF HIS LUNCH WANTED TO SING, THAT WAS FINE.
BUT JUST AS HE WA ABOUT TO POUNCE, LUCIFER HEARD SOMETHING...
CREEEAK
?
IT WAS GUS!

"LUCIFER REALIZED THIS WAS A TRICK TO GET THE BEADS... SO HE QUICKLY SAT BACK DOWN ON THEM"
AND THEN WATCHED GUS SCRAMBLE BACK INTO THE WALL.
BUT HOW WOULD LUCIFER CATCH JAQ WITHOUT LETTING GUS TAKE THE BEADS? HE THOUGHT ABOUT IT... AND THEN BEGAN TO SLIDE TOWARDS JAQ, DRAGGING THE BEADS ALONG!
OH!
MEANWHILE, JAQ KEPT HUMMING AWAY AND GOING ABOUT HIS WORK...
...AS THOUGH HE HADN'T A CARE IN THE WORLD.

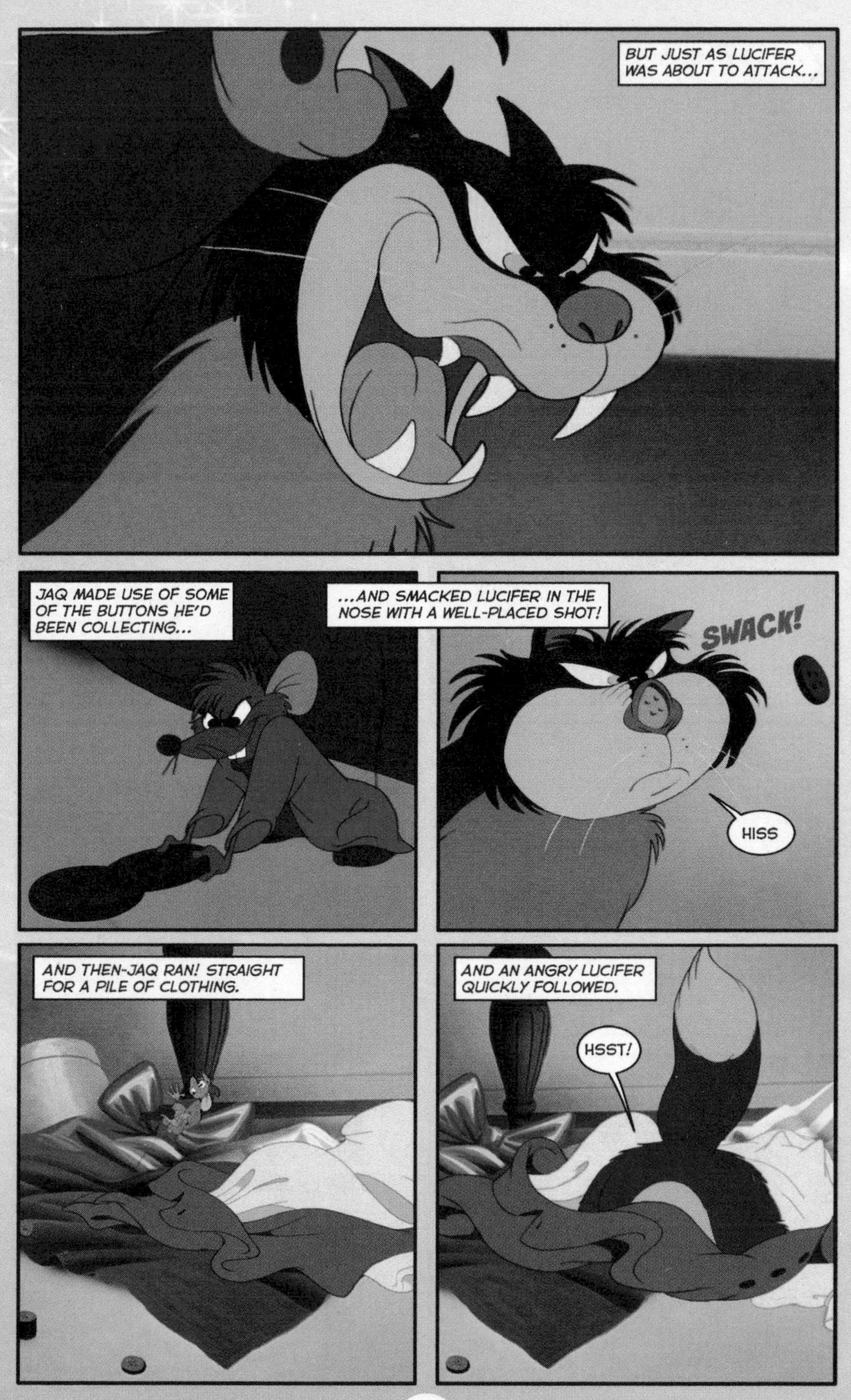
BUT JUST AS LUCIFER WAS ABOUT TO ATTACK...
JAQ MADE USE OF SOME OF THE BUTTONS HE'D BEEN COLLECTING...
...AND SMACKED LUCIFER IN THE NOSE WITH A WELL-PLACED SHOT!
SWACK!
HISS
AND THEN-JAQ RAN! STRAIGHT FOR A PILE OF CLOTHING.
AND AN ANGRY LUCIFER QUICKLY FOLLOWED.
HSST!

HO HO!
GUS HAS MADE HIS WAY TO THE BEADS WHILE LUCIFER WAS DISTRACTED, SEARCHING FOR JAQ.
BUT THE DISTRACTION COULDN'T LAST FOREVER.
ESPECIALLY WHEN GUS WAS STILL SO CLUMSY!
KSNASH
SO JAQ GOT LUCIFER'S ATTENTION AGAIN --
BOP
...AND DOVE RIGHT BACK INTO THE PILE OF CLOTHES.

JAQ QUICKLY ESCAPED THROUGH THE SLEEVE OF A NIGHTGOWN...
...AND RAN OFF TO JOIN GUS.
LUCIFER WAS STUCK IN THE SLEEVE TRYING TO FOLLOW, BUT INCHED TOWARD THE MICE LIKE A GIANT WORM.
EVEN TRAPPED, LUCIFER ALMOST GOT THEM.
BUT ONLY ALMOST!

MEANWHILE, BACK IN THE LOFT, THE OTHER MICE AND BIRDS MERRILY WORK ON CINDERELLA'S DRESS.
THERE, JUST RIGHT!
AND NOW...
FROM MEASURING...

SNIP
TO CUTTING...
HO HO HO!
SNIP SNIP
TO SEWING.
THE GOWN WAS COMING TOGETHER BEAUTIFULLY.

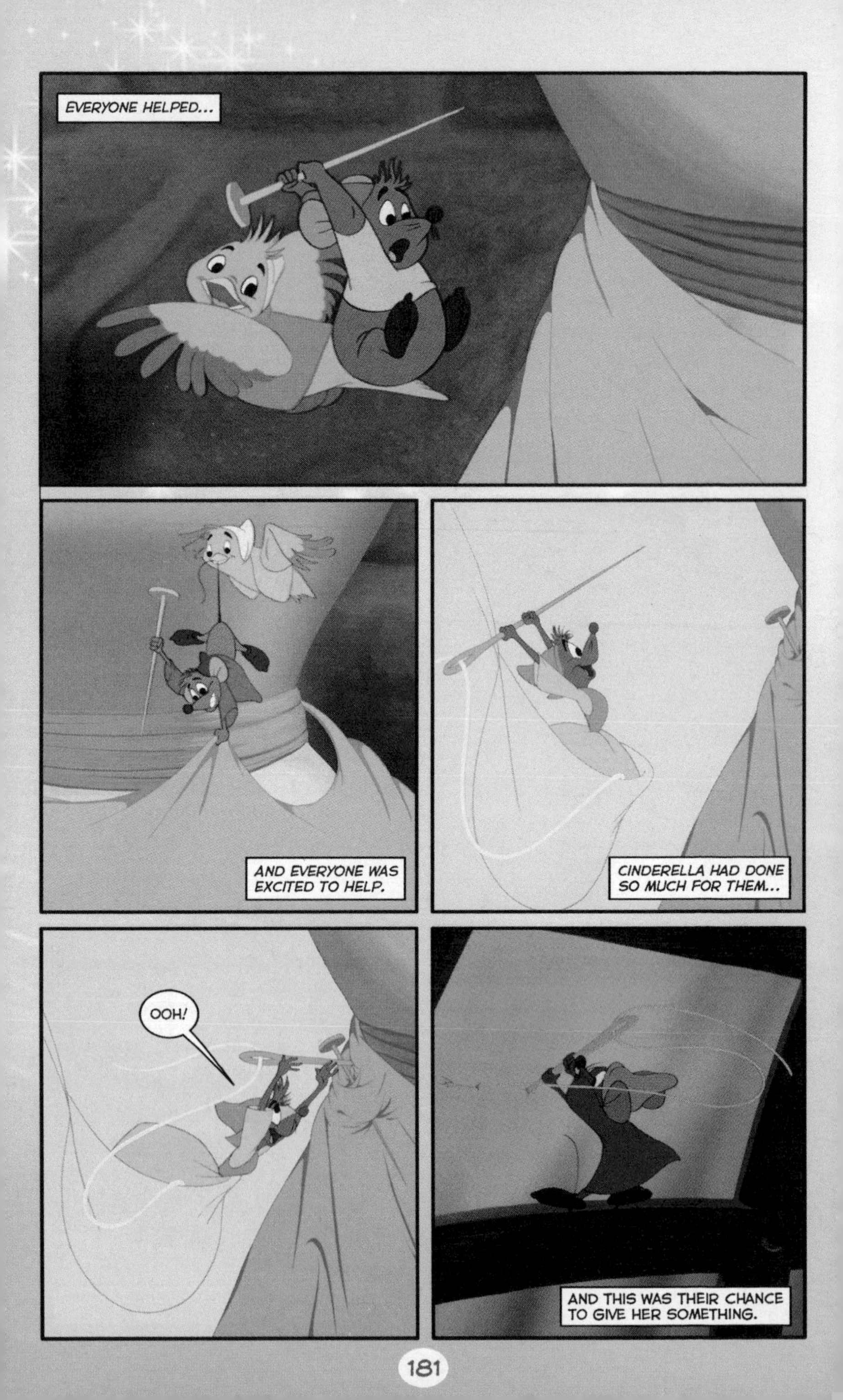
EVERYONE HELPED...
AND EVERYONE WAS EXCITED TO HELP.
CINDERELLA HAD DONE SO MUCH FOR THEM...
OOH!
AND THIS WAS THEIR CHANCE TO GIVE HER SOMETHING.

AND THAT IT WOULD BE A SURPRISE WAS THE BEST PART!
TWEET-TWEET!
OKAY!
...5, 6, 7, 8!

READY!
ALL RIGHT!
HEAVE, HO! HEAVE, HO!
HEAVE, HO!

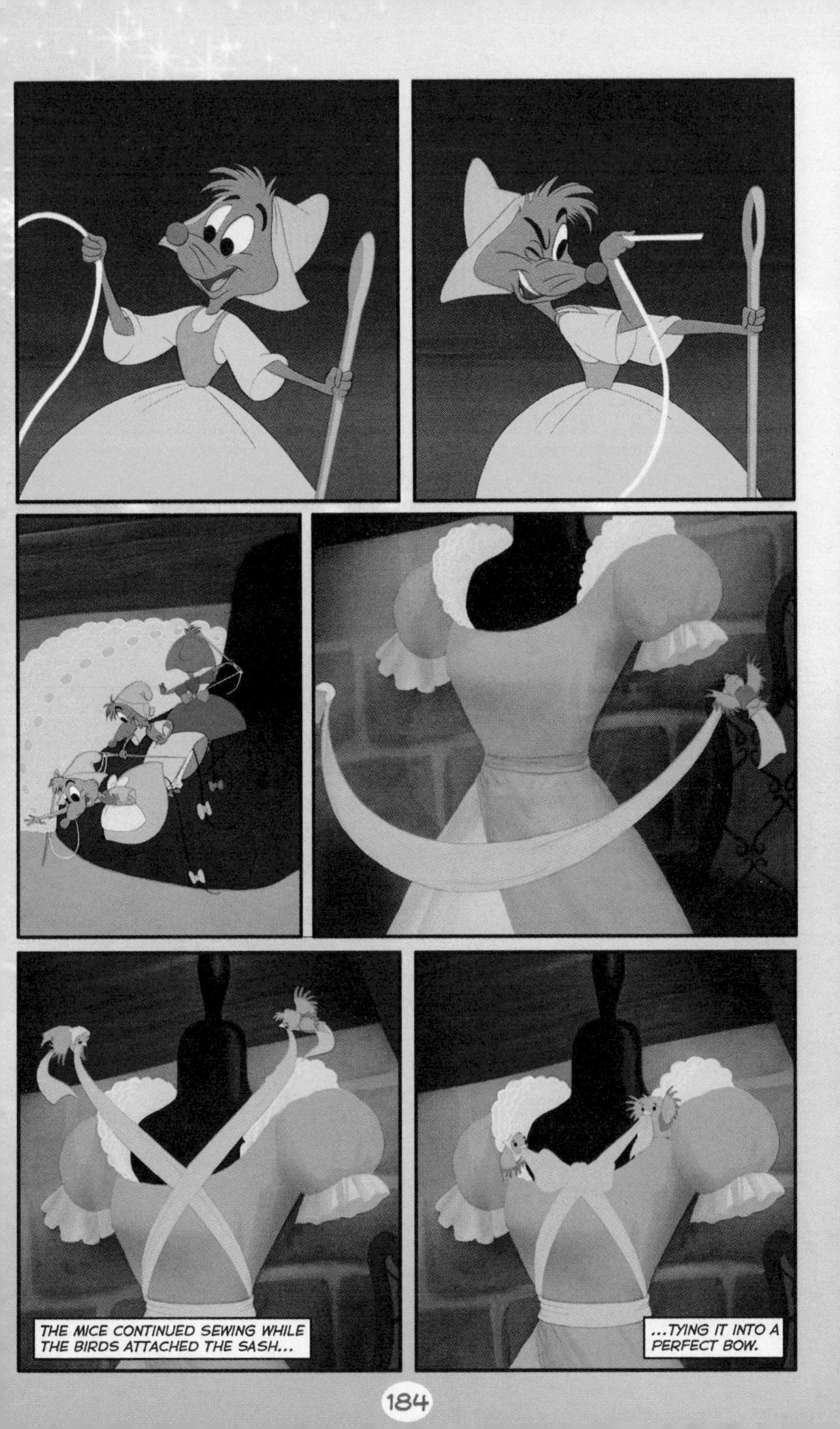
THE MICE CONTINUED SEWING WHILE THE BIRDS ATTACHED THE SASH...
...TYING IT INTO A PERFECT BOW.

SNIP
WELL... ALMOST PERFECT.
THEY'D EVEN RESTRUNG THE BEADS INTO A NICE NECKLACE.
CINDERELLA WAS GOING TO BE SO HAPPY!

LATER...
THE DUKE DISPATCHES CARRIAGES FROM THE PALACE...
...TO MAKE SURE THE ELIGIBLE LADIES OF THE KINGDOM FIND THEIR WAY SAFELY TO THE BALL.
CINDERELLA WATCHES THE CARRIAGE PULL UP TO HER FAMILY CHATEAU AND SIGHS...

YES?
KNOCK
KNOCK
THE CARRIAGE IS HERE.
AH.
WHY, CINDERELLA! YOU'RE NOT READY, CHILD.
I'M NOT GOING.

NOT GOING?
OH, WHAT A SHAME.
BUT OF COURSE THERE WILL BE OTHER TIMES --
YES.
GOOD NIGHT.

OH, WELL. WHATS A ROYAL BALL?
AFTER ALL, I SUPPOSE IT WOULD BE FRIGHTFULLY DULL.
AND... AND BORING! AND COMPLETELY --
--COMPLETELY WONDERFUL.
AND THEN, CINDERELLA HEARS A NOISE...
WHAT...?

AND THAT'S WHEN SHE SAW IT.

...HER DRESS.

SURPRISE!

SURPRISE!

UH, DUH - HAPPY BIRTHDAY!

NO, NO!

WHY, I NEVER DREAMED THAT --
IT'S SUCH A SURPRISE!
HOW CAN I EVER -
OH! THANK YOU!
THANK YOU SO MUCH!

A FEW MINUTES LATER, DOWNSTAIRS...
NOW, REMEMBER; WHEN YOU'RE PRESENTED TO HIS HIGHNESS, BE SURE TO--
WAIT!!
PLEASE, WAIT FOR ME!
ISN'T IT LOVELY? DO YOU LIKE IT?
DO YOU THINK IT WILL DO?

CINDERELLA! OH, MOTHER, SHE CAN'T!
YOU WOULDN'T - YOU CAN'T LET HER!
GIRLS, PLEASE!
AFTER ALL, WE DID MAKE A BARGAIN.
DIDN'T WE, CINDERELLA?
AND I NEVER GO BACK ON MY WORD.

HOW VERY CLEVER. THESE BEADS. THEY GIVE IT JUST THE RIGHT TOUCH.
DON'T YOU THINK SO, DRIZELLA?
NO, I DON'T I THINK SHE'S --
OH! WHY YOU LITTLE THIEF!
THEY'RE MY BEADS - GIVE THEM HERE!
OH, NO!

THAT'S MY SASH!
SHE'S WEARING MY SASH - SHE CAN'T!
OH, NO, PLEASE, NO!
AND THAT'S MY RIBBON, YOU THIEF!
GIVE IT HERE!

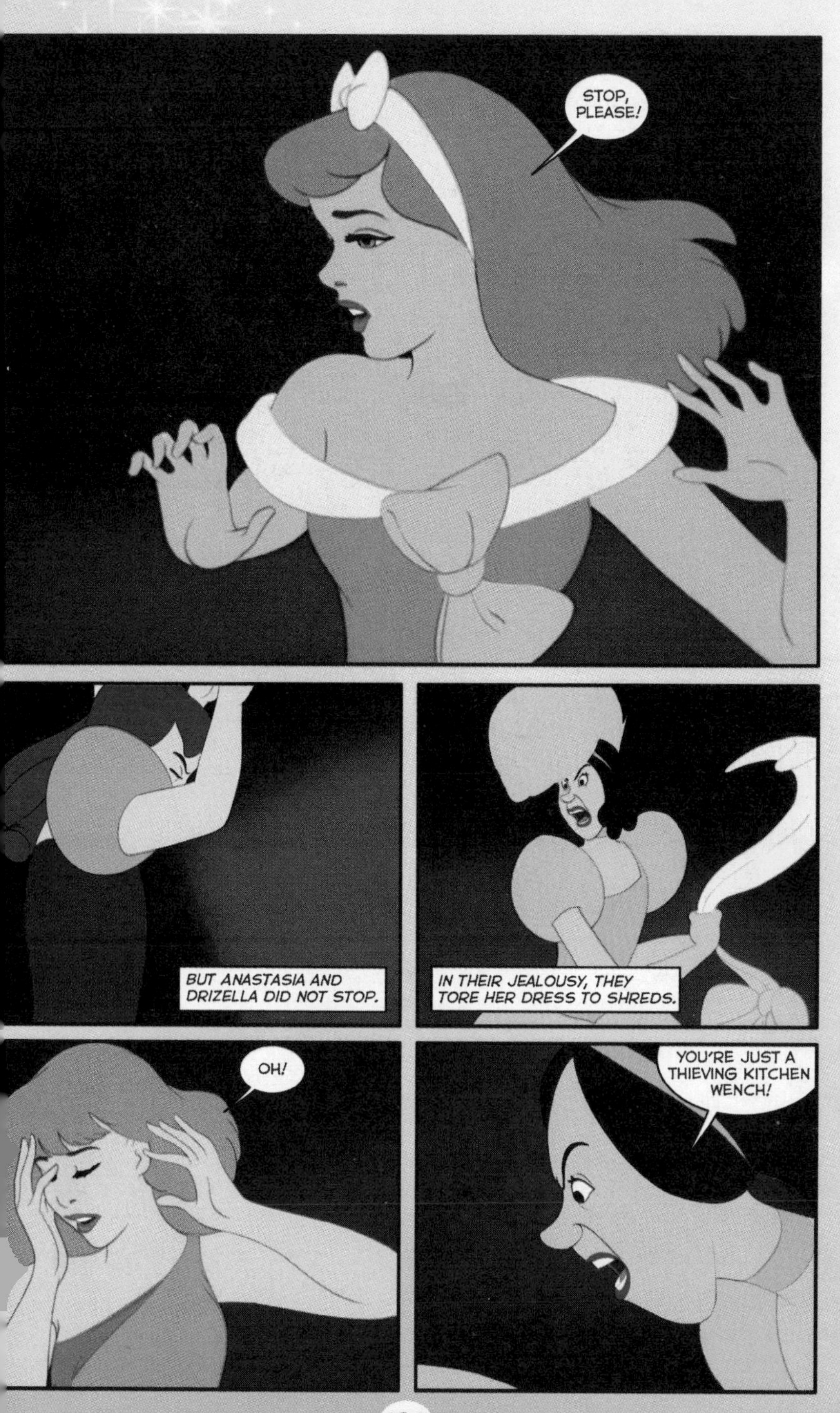
STOP, PLEASE!
BUT ANASTASIA AND DRIZELLA DID NOT STOP.
IN THEIR JEALOUSY, THEY TORE HER DRESS TO SHREDS.
OH!
YOU'RE JUST A THIEVING KITCHEN WENCH!

GIRLS, GIRLS.
THAT'S QUITE ENOUGH.
HURRY ALONG NOW, BOTH OF YOU.
I WON'T HAVE YOU UPSETTING YOURSELVES.

CINDERELLA...
GOODNIGHT.
SOB!

HEARTBROKEN, CINDERELLA RUNS.
THROUGH THE CHATEAU, OUT INTO THE YARD...
PAST THE STABLES...
...TO THE FOUNTAIN SHE AND HER FATHER HAD LOVED.
AND THERE, SHE SOBBED.

HER ANIMAL FRIENDS GATHERED AROUND, HEARTBROKEN AS WELL.
THEY WANTED DESPERATELY TO HELP...
BUT KNEW THERE WAS NOTHING THEY COULD DO.
IT'S JUST NO USE...

SUDDENLY, SPARKLING LIGHTS APPEARED...
...AND BEGAN TO DANCE IN THE AIR.
I CAN'T BELIEVE - NOT ANYMORE...
THE LIGHTS DANCED THEIR WAY TOWARDS CINDERELLA...

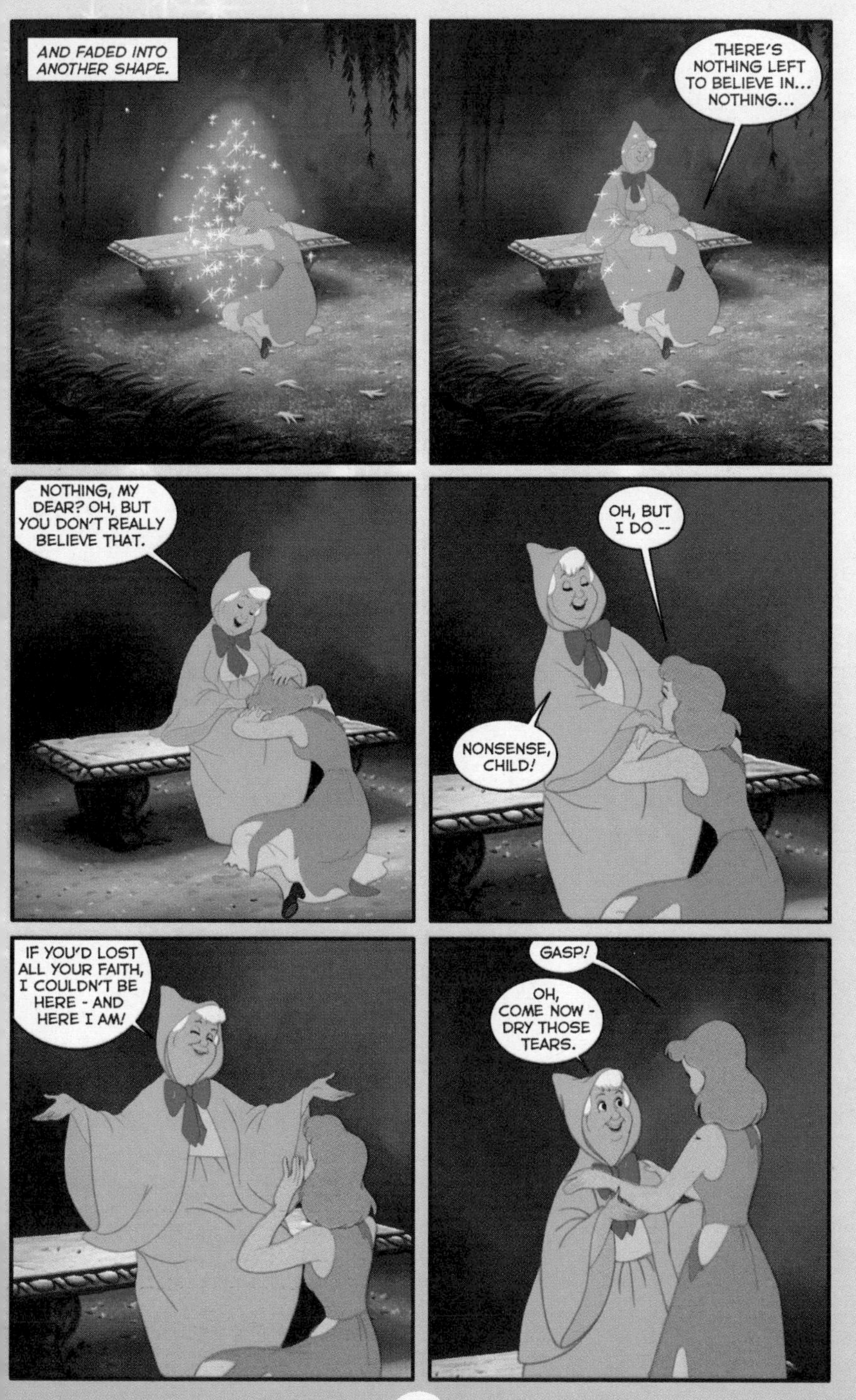
AND FADED INTO ANOTHER SHAPE.
THERE'S NOTHING LEFT TO BELIEVE IN... NOTHING...
NOTHING, MY DEAR? OH, BUT YOU DON'T REALLY BELIEVE THAT.
OH, BUT I DO --
NONSENSE, CHILD!
IF YOU'D LOST ALL YOUR FAITH, I COULDN'T BE HERE - AND HERE I AM!
GASP!
OH, COME NOW - DRY THOSE TEARS.

YOU CAN'T GO TO THE BALL LOOKING LIKE THAT!
...THE BALL?
OH, BUT I'M NOT --
OF COURSE YOU ARE!
BUT WE'LL HAVE TO HURRY --
BECAUSE EVEN MIRACLES TAKE A LITTLE TIME.

MIRACLES?
MM-HMM--
WATCH!
NOW WHAT IN THE WORLD DID I DO WITH THAT MAGIC WAND?
I WAS SURE THAT I - THAT'S STRANGE.
MAGIC WAND?
WHY THEN YOU MUST BE--
YOUR FAIRY GODMOTHER? OF COURSE!

NOW WHERE IS THAT WAND? I --
OH! I FORGOT.
I'D PUT IT AWAY.
swish
GASP!
LOOKIT WHAT SHE DID!
UH, DUH - . HOW SHE DO IT?

NOW, LET'S SEE... HMM.
I'D SAY THE FIRST THING YOU NEED IS--
A PUMPKIN!
BUT, UH, A PUMPKIN?
OH YES! NOW, AH...
WHAT WERE THE MAGIC WORDS...

OH, YES!
AH, HERE WE GO NOW...
BIBBIDI
THE WORDS CINDERELLA'S FAIRY GODMOTHER SPEAK DON'T SOUND PARTICULARLY ANCIENT...
BOBBIDI
...OR ALL THAT MYSTERIOUS...
...BUT THEIR EFFECT IS DAZZLING ALL THE SAME!
BOO!
AND WITH THOSE WORDS, THE FAIRY GODMOTHER'S WAND CAME TO LIFE AND BREATHED MAGIC INTO AIR...

MAGIC THAT MADE ITS WAY TO THE FINEST PUMPKIN IN A NEARBY PATCH...
...AND BROUGHT IT TO LIFE.
THE PUMPKIN JUMPED AND BOUNCED, PULLED FORTH BY THE MAGIC, USING ITS VINES AS LEGS!
NOW I'LL REALLY SHOW YOU SOMETHING!
WITH ANOTHER FLASH OF MAGIC...
THE PUMPKIN AND ITS VINES BEGAN TO GROW.

BIBBIDI
BOBBIDI
BOO!
OH, IT'S BEAUTIFUL!
OH, LOOKY LOOKY!

YES, ISN'T IT?
NOW, WITH AN ELEGANT COACH LIKE THAT, OF COURSE, WE'LL SIMPLY HAVE TO HAVE --
AHEM.
-- MICE!
?!?
MICE??
OH, THIS REALLY IS NICE.
WHY, WE'LL HAVE A COACH AND FOUR WHEN WE'RE THROUGH!
JUST A WAVE OF MY STICK, AND TO FINISH THE TRICK --

BIBBIDI
BOBBIDI
BOO!
GRACIOUS, WHAT DID I DO? I WAS SURE THERE WERE FOUR THERE... THERE SHOULD BE ONE MORE...
OH! THERE YOU ARE.

BIBBIDI
BOBBIDI
BOO!
MROW?
FWAAASH
?!?

SNORT.
WHINNEY HEEHEEHEE!
MRROOW!!!
SPLASH
HISS! WHEEZE!
OH, POOR LUCIFER!
HEE HEE HEE!

SERVES HIM RIGHT, I'D SAY. NOW, UM... WHERE WERE WE?
OH, GOODNESS, YES!
YOU CAN'T GO TO THE BALL WITHOUT --
-- A HORSE!
A... ANOTHER ONE?
BUT TONIGHT, FOR A CHANGE --
YOU'LL HANDLE THE REINS!

AND SIT IN THE DRIVER'S SEAT, TOO!
INSTEAD OF A HORSE, YOU'LL BE A COACHMAN, OF COURSE!
BIBBIDI BOBBIDI BOO!

WELL, THAT DOES IT, I GUESS! EXCEPT FOR, OH YES!

THE FINISHING TOUCH.

AND THAT'S YOU!

YES, BRUNO, THAT'S RIGHT!
YOU'LL BE A FOOTMAN TONIGHT!

BIBBIDI
BOBBIDI
BOO!
WELL HOP IN, MY DEAR!

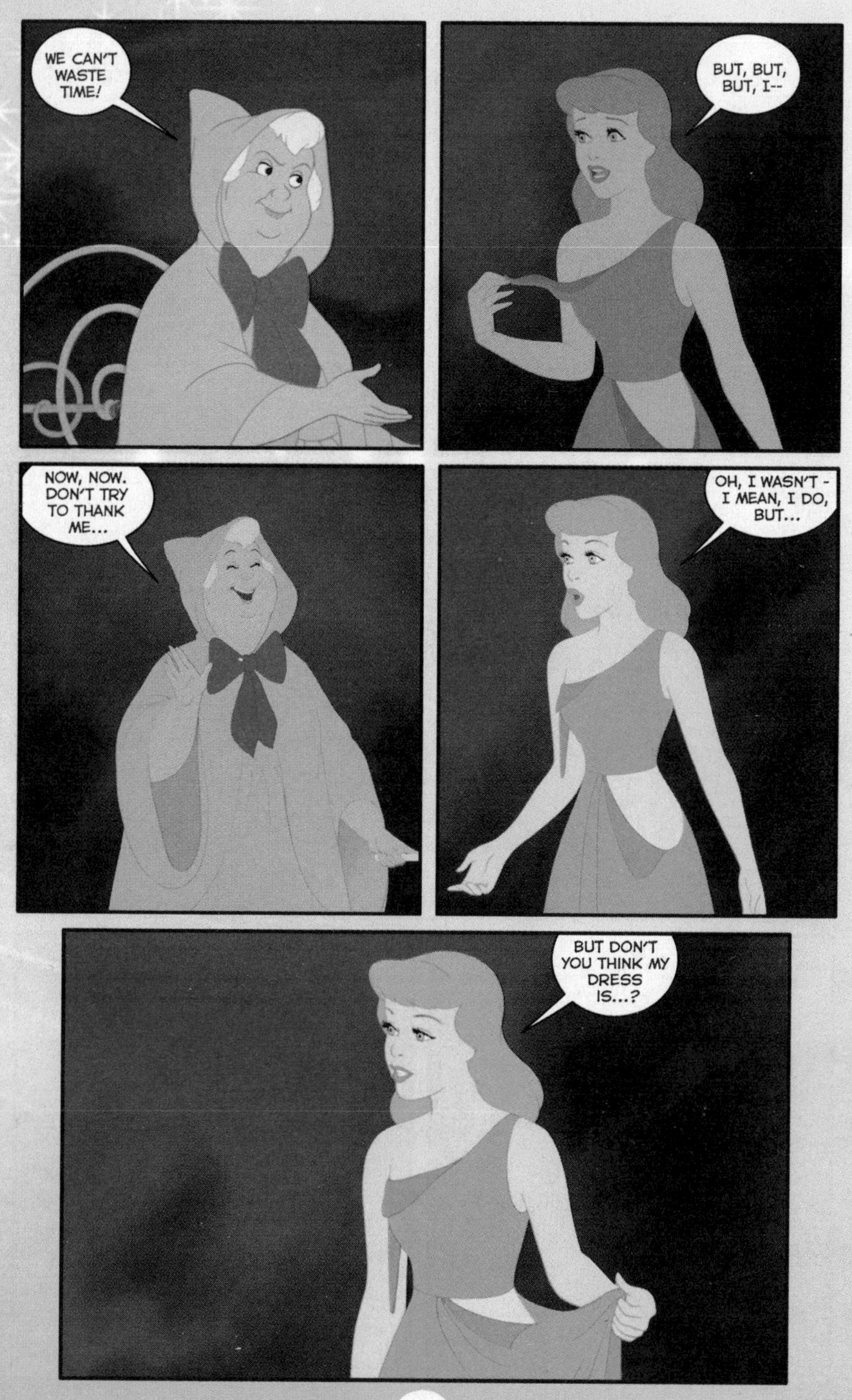
WE CAN'T WASTE TIME!
BUT, BUT, BUT, I--
NOW, NOW. DON'T TRY TO THANK ME...
OH, I WASN'T - I MEAN, I DO, BUT...
BUT DON'T YOU THINK MY DRESS IS...?

YES, IT'S LOVELY, DEAR.
LOV--
--GOOD HEAVENS, CHILD! YOU CAN'T GO IN THAT!
NOW, LET'S SEE, DEAR... YOUR SIZE...
SHADE OF YOUR EYES, AND... MM-HMM.

SOMETHING SIMPLE --
BUT DARING, TOO!
JUST LEAVE IT TO ME, OH! WHAT A GOWN THIS WILL BE.
BIBBIDI BOBBIDI...

BIBBIDI BOBBIDI--
--BIBBIDI--
--BOO!

AGAIN THE FAIRY MAGIC SPARKLED IN THE AIR, TRANSFORMING CINDERELLA'S RAGS INTO A WONDERFUL GOWN FOR THE BALL.
OH!
OH, IT'S A BEAUTIFUL DRESS!
HAVE YOU EVER SEEN SUCH A BEAUTIFUL DRESS?
AND LOOK! GLASS SLIPPERS!

WHY, IT'S LIKE A DREAM!
A WONDERFUL DREAM COME TRUE!
YES, MY CHILD. BUT LIKE ALL DREAMS, WELL, I'M AFRAID THIS CAN'T LAST FOREVER.
YOU'LL HAVE ONLY 'TIL MIDNIGHT, AND THEN --
MIDNIGHT? OH, THANK YOU.
OH, NOW, NOW JUST A MINUTE - YOU MUST UNDERSTAND, MY DEAR.
ON THE STROKE OF TWELVE, THE SPELL WILL BE BROKEN, AND EVERYTHING WILL BE AS IT WAS BEFORE.
OH, I UNDERSTAND BUT - IT'S MORE THAN I EVER HOPED FOR.
BLESS YOU, MY CHILD.

GOODNESS, ME! IT'S GETTING LATE!
HURRY UP, DEAR, THE BALL CAN'T WAIT! HAVE A GOOD TIME!
DANCE! BE GAY!
NOW OFF YOU GO, YOU'RE ON YOUR WAY!
AS THE COACH PULLED AWAY, THE FAIRY GODMOTHER WAVED GOODNIGHT...
...VANISHING INTO SPARKLING LIGHTS SOON AFTER.

THE COACH WAS WONDERFUL...

...SWIFTLY MAKING ITS WAY ACROSS THE COUNTRYSIDE...

AND THROUGH THE TOWN...

...ON ITS WAY TO THE PALACE.

MEANWHILE, AT THE ROYAL BALL...
THE PRINCE IS BEING INTRODUCED TO...WELL, ALL OF THE ELIGIBLE LADIES OF THE KINGDOM.
THE PRINCESS FREDERICA EUGENIE DE LA FONTAINE.

M'AMSELLE AUGUSTINA DUBOIS, DAUGHTER OF GENERAL PIERRE DUBOIS.
AND WITH EACH NEW INTRODUCTION...
THE KING LOOKS ON, WITH HOPEFUL EYES.

AHHHH!

THE BOY ISN'T COOPERATING.

M'MSELLE LEONORA MERCEDES DE LA TORRE, DAUGHTER OF COLONEL AND MADAM DE LA TORRE.

AGAIN, THE KING GETS HIS HOPES UP...

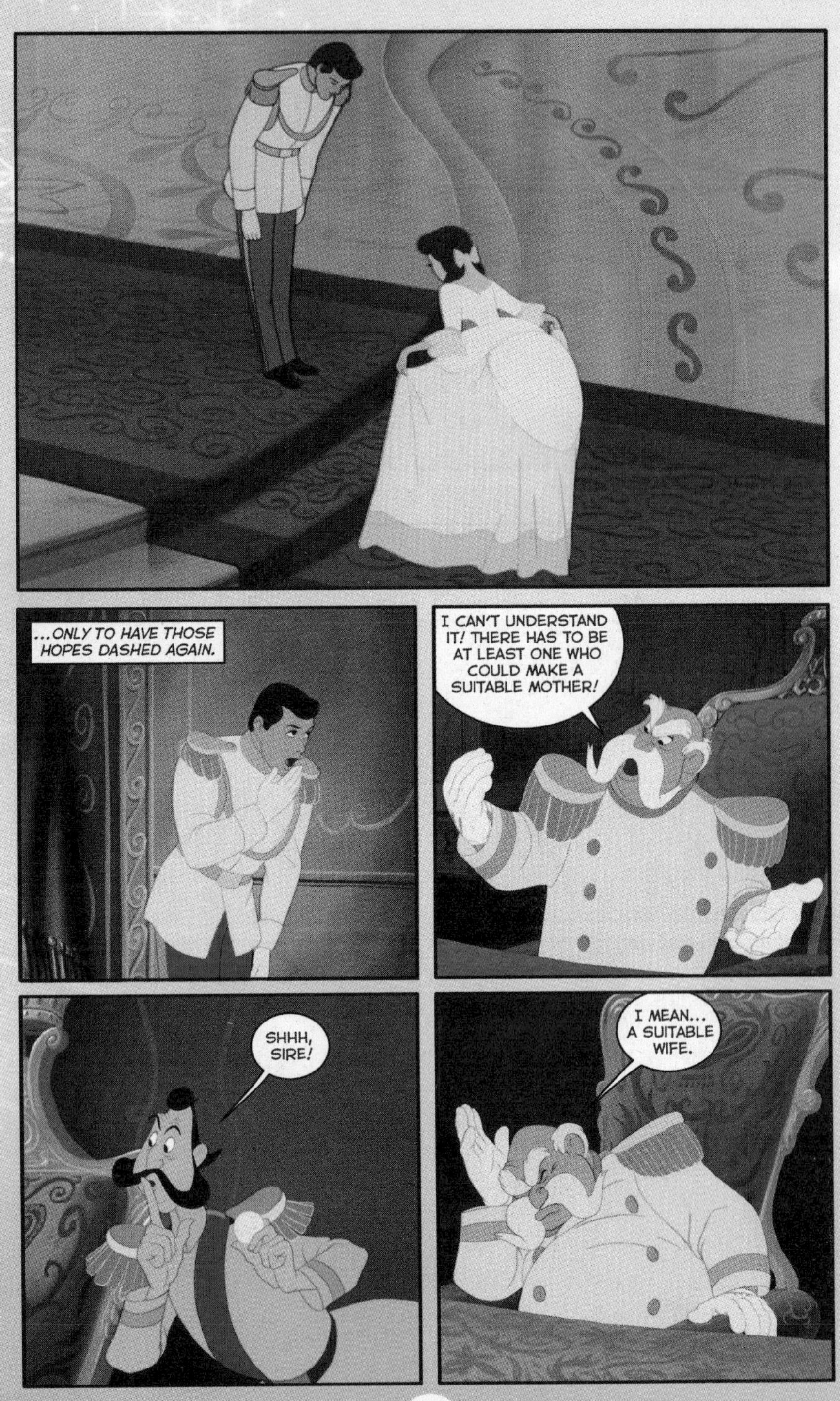
...ONLY TO HAVE THOSE HOPES DASHED AGAIN.
I CAN'T UNDERSTAND IT! THERE HAS TO BE AT LEAST ONE WHO COULD MAKE A SUITABLE MOTHER!
SHHH, SIRE!
I MEAN... A SUITABLE WIFE.

AND THEN, FINALLY...

CINDERELLA ARRIVES.
THE GUARDS SEE HER, BUT MAKE NO MOVE TO STOP HER.
AFTER ALL, SHE WAS INVITED.

THE MADEMOISELLES DRIZELLA AND ANASTASIA TREMAINE...
DAUGHTERS OF LADY TREMAINE.
AH, I GIVE UP.
EVEN I COULDN'T EXPECT THE BOY TO --

WELL, IF I MAY SAY SO YOUR MAJESTY, I DID TRY TO WARN YOU.

BUT YOU, SIRE, ARE INCURABLY ROMANTIC

HA HA!

NO DOUBT YOU SAW THE WHOLE PRETTY PICTURE IN DETAIL.

THE YOUNG PRINCE, BOWING TO THE ASSEMBLY.
BUT SUDDENLY HE STOPS.
HE LOOKS UP.
FOR LO, THERE SHE STANDS, THE GIRL OF HIS DREAMS!
WHO SHE IS OR WHENCE SHE CAME, HE KNOWS NOT.
NOR DOES HE CARE.

FOR HIS HEART TELLS HIM THAT HERE...
HERE IS THE MAID PREDESTINED TO BE HIS BRIDE.
A PRETTY PLOT FOR FAIRY TALES, SIRE...

BUT IN REAL LIFE?
OH, HO, HO, HO, NO. IT WAS FOREDOOMED TO FAILURE.
FAILURE, EH?
TAKE A LOOK AT THAT, YOU POMPOUS WINDBAG!
HA HA HA!

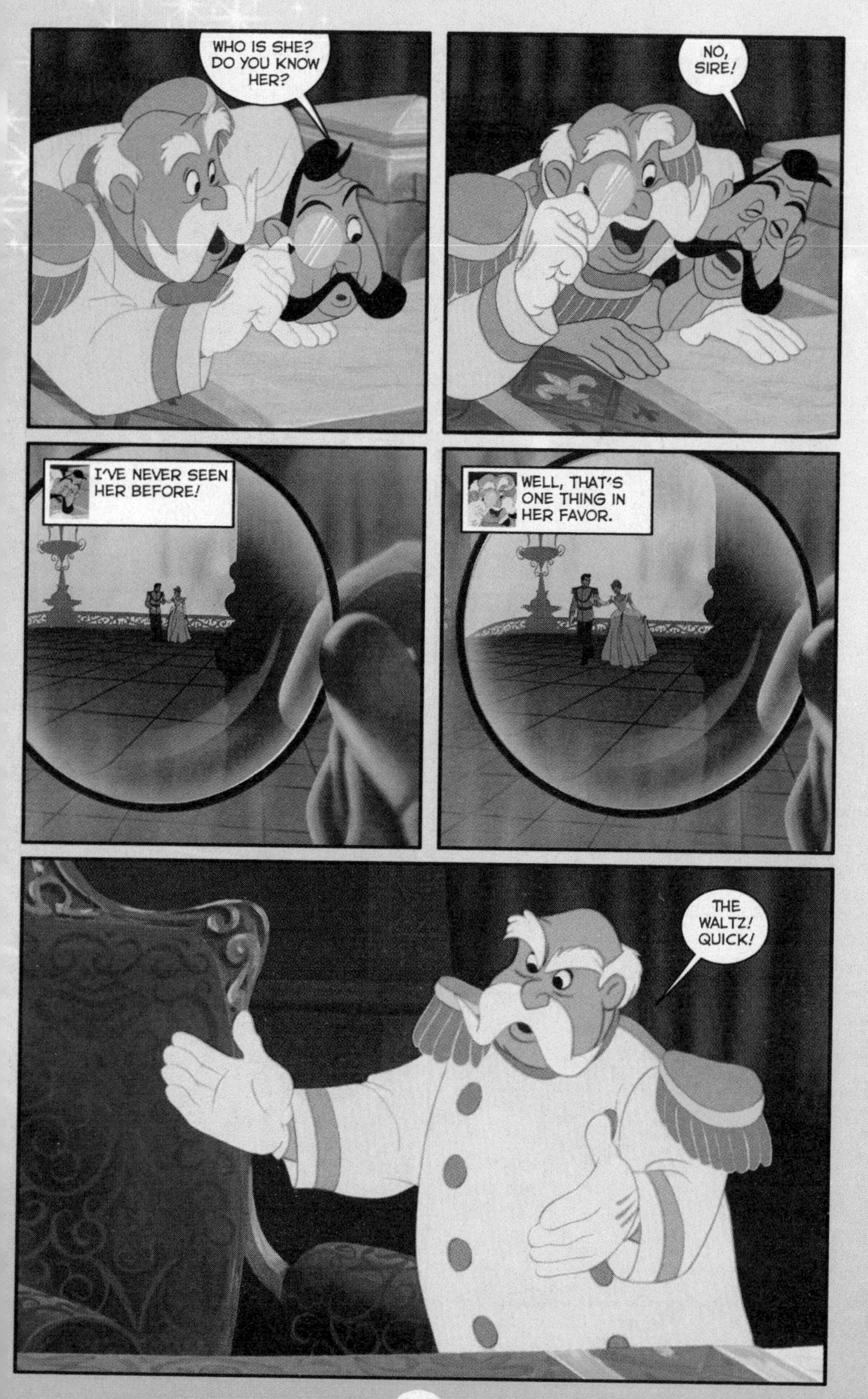
WHO IS SHE? DO YOU KNOW HER?
NO, SIRE!
I'VE NEVER SEEN HER BEFORE!
WELL, THAT'S ONE THING IN HER FAVOR.
THE WALTZ! QUICK!

THE WALTZ!
AND NOW, THE LIGHTS.
YOU THERE! THE LIGHTS -
WHOOP!
THE LIGHTS!

AS THE MUSIC FILLED THE CHAMBER, CINDERELLA AND THE PRINCE TOOK TO THE FLOOR AND DANCED...
...AS IF IT WERE ONLY THE TWO OF THEM.

HA-HA, FAILURE, EH?
AH, YES.
'HA HA HA.'
WELL, NOW FOR A GOOD NIGHT'S SLEEP.
OH, QUITE SO, SIRE. I BELIEVE I, TOO --
YOU WILL STAY RIGHT HERE.
SEE THEY'RE NOT DISTURBED...

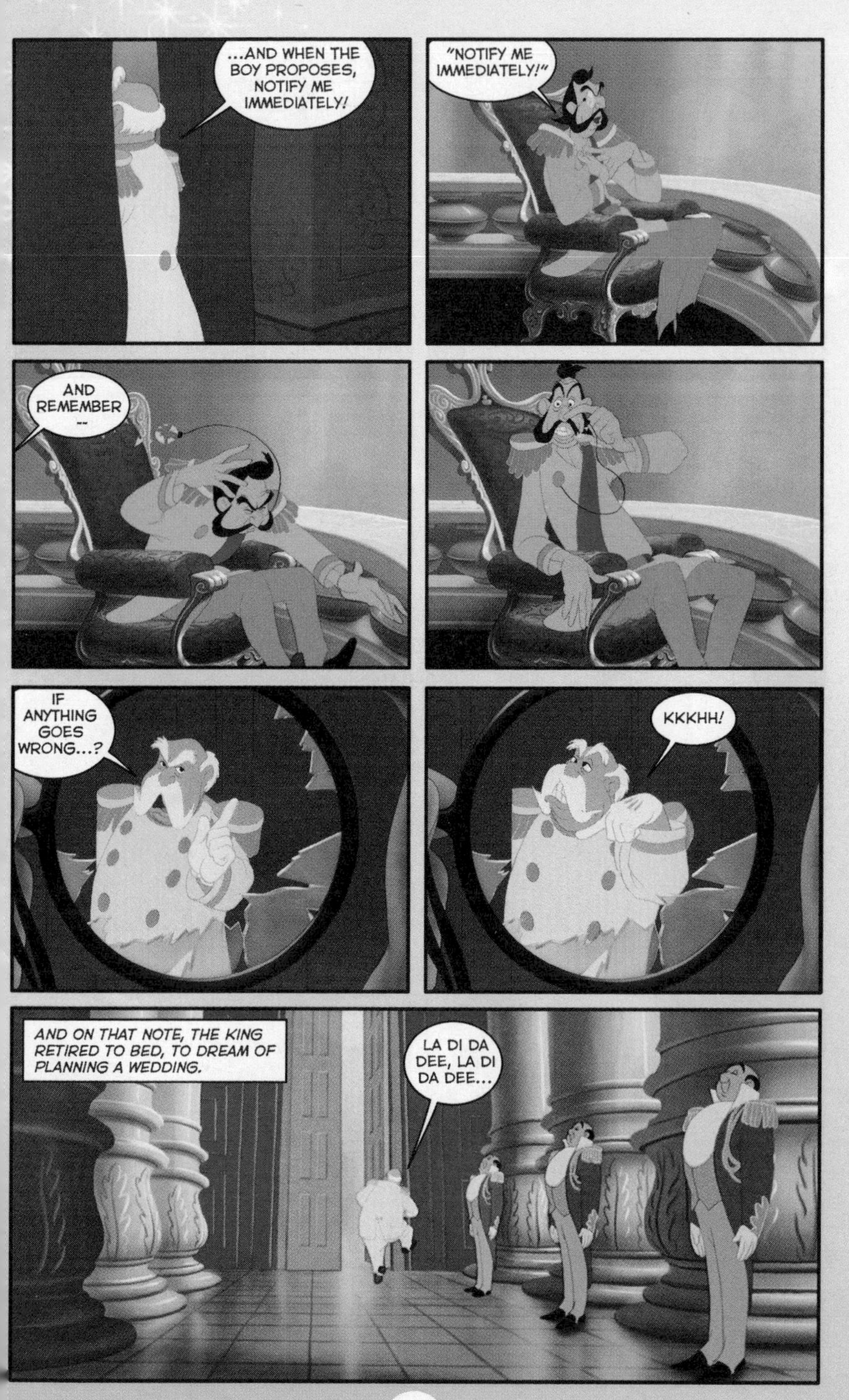
...AND WHEN THE BOY PROPOSES, NOTIFY ME IMMEDIATELY!
"NOTIFY ME IMMEDIATELY!"
AND REMEMBER --
IF ANYTHING GOES WRONG...?
KKKHH!
AND ON THAT NOTE, THE KING RETIRED TO BED, TO DREAM OF PLANNING A WEDDING.
LA DI DA DEE, LA DI DA DEE...

MEANWHILE, BACK IN THE BALLROOM...
BUT WHO IS SHE, MOTHER?
DO WE KNOW HER?
THE PRINCE CERTAINLY SEEMS TO --
--BUT I KNOW I'VE NEVER SEEN HER.
NOR I, BUT SHE CERTAINLY IS --
WAIT.
THERE IS SOMETHING FAMILIAR ABOUT HER.

AS CINDERELLA AND THE PRINCE DANCE OUT OF PUBLIC VIEW...
THE LADY TREMAINE MOVES IN AND TRIES TO GET A CLOSER LOOK.
WHY IS THIS GIRL FAMILIAR?
BUT BEFORE SHE CAN GET TOO CLOSE... A CURTAIN DROPS.
OH!
AHEM.

CINDERELLA, ON THE OTHER HAND, DIDN'T EVEN NOTICE THAT HER STEPMOTHER HAD BEEN TRYING TO FOLLOW HER.
SHE AND THE PRINCE ARE LOST IN THE DANCE...
...AND ONLY HAVE EYES FOR ONE ANOTHER.

THEIR DANCE BECOMES A ROMANTIC STROLL IN THE GARDEN...
...THAT BECOME A DANCE AGAIN.

TRULY, LOVE IS
IN THE AIR.
BUT, JUST AS CINDERELLA AND THE
PRINCE SHARE THEIR FIRST KISS...
THE CLOCK BEGINS TO CHIME.
BONG

OH MY GOODNESS!
WHAT'S THE MATTER?
IT'S MIDNIGHT!
YES, SO IT IS, BUT WHY --
GOODBYE!
NO, NO WAIT -- YOU CAN'T GO NOW, IT'S ONLY--
OH NO, I MUST! PLEASE, I MUST!
BUT WHY?

THE PRINCE.
I HAVEN'T MET THE PRINCE.
THE PRINCE? BUT DIDN'T YOU KNOW THAT --
BONG
GOODBYE!
NO, WAIT!

COME BACK!
PLEASE COME BACK!
I DON'T EVEN KNOW YOUR NAME, HOW WILL I FIND YOU?
WAIT, PLEASE!

GOODBYE!

EH?

BUT --
I SAY, YOUNG LADY!

WAIT!
THE PRINCE CONTINUES TO CHASE CINDERELLA --
OH, THE PRINCE!
THERE HE IS!
-- BUT HIS PATH IS QUICKLY BLOCKED BY A GROUP OF YOUNG WOMEN STILL HOPING TO CATCH HIS EYE.

CINDERELLA RUNS AS FAST AS SHE
CAN TO MAKE IT BACK TO HER COACH...

SO FAST, THAT SHE LOSES
ONE OF HER GLASS SLIPPERS
ON THE STAIRCASE.

BUT SHE CAN'T STOP TO RETRIEVE IT - THE DUKE IS FAST APPROACHING, AND THE SPELL IS ABOUT TO BREAK!
WAIT!
MADEMOISELLE!
SENORITA?
YOU MUST COME BACK, PLEASE!

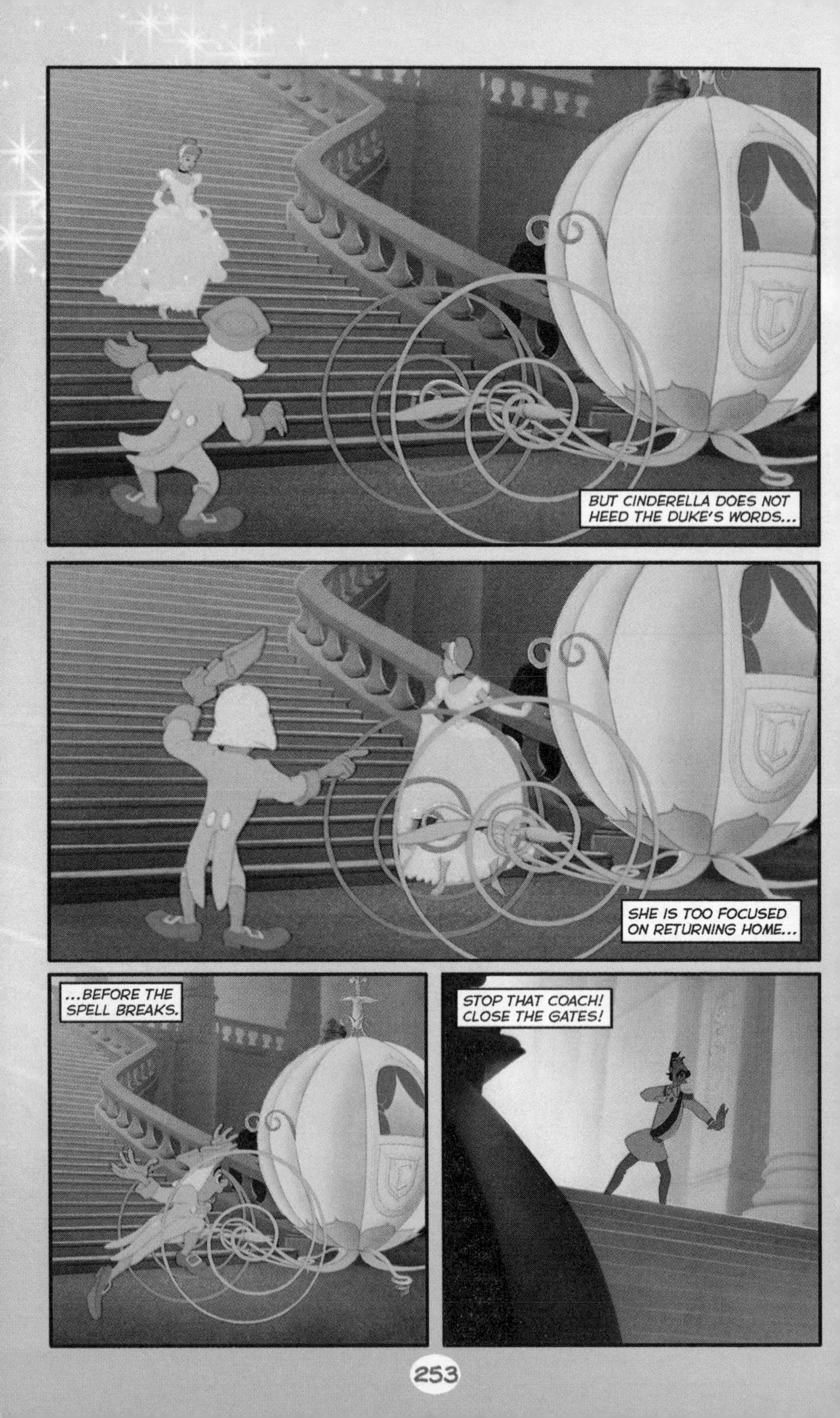
BUT CINDERELLA DOES NOT HEED THE DUKE'S WORDS...
SHE IS TOO FOCUSED ON RETURNING HOME...
...BEFORE THE SPELL BREAKS.
STOP THAT COACH! CLOSE THE GATES!

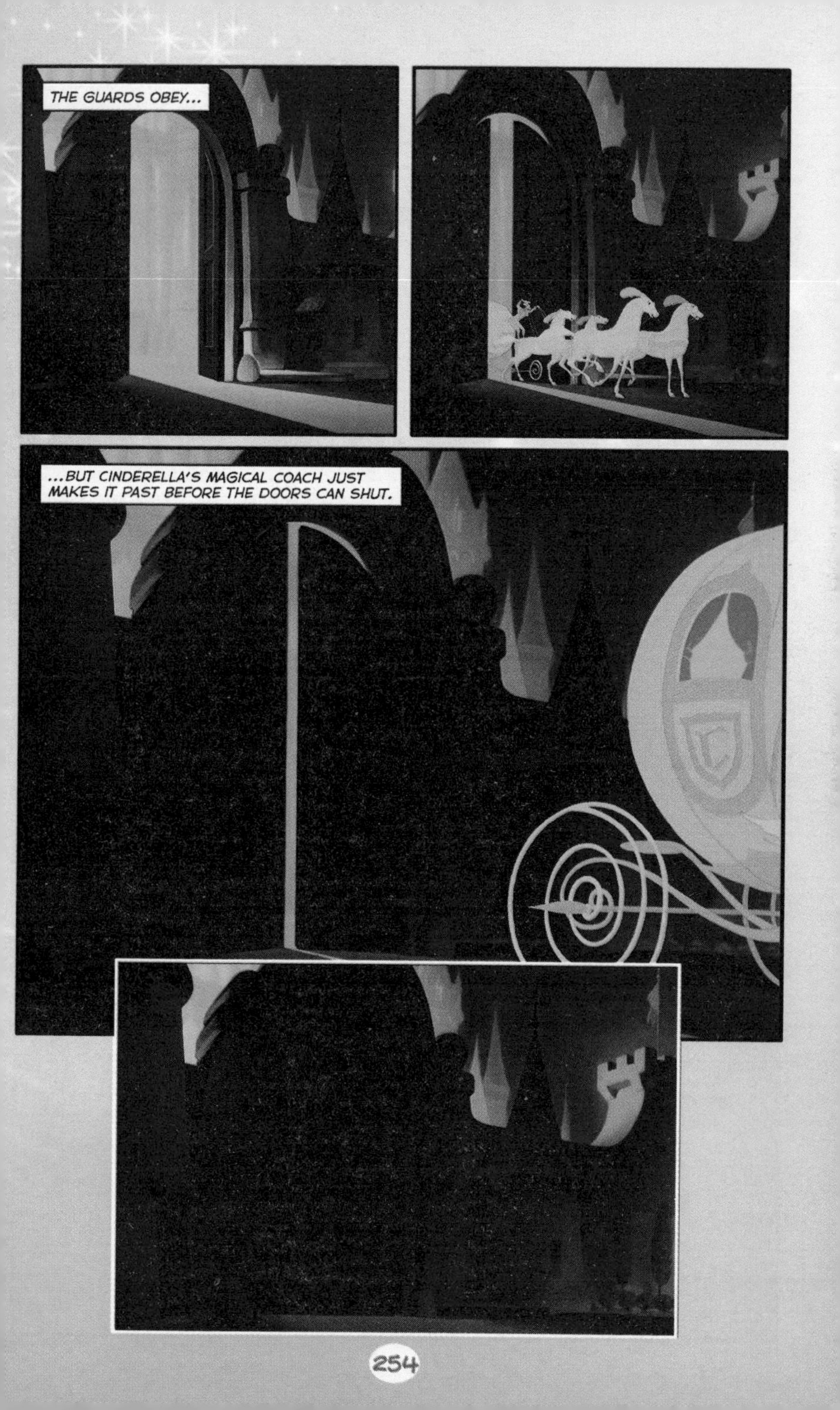
THE GUARDS OBEY...
...BUT CINDERELLA'S MAGICAL COACH JUST MAKES IT PAST BEFORE THE DOORS CAN SHUT.

OH!
FOLLOW THAT COACH!!
OPEN THE GATES!!

THE CASTLE RIDERS SET OFF AFTER CINDERELLA'S COACH...
...AND THE CLOCK CONTINUES TO CHIME MIDNIGHT.
BONG
THROUGH THE COUNTRYSIDE THE COACH RACES...

BONG
BUT THE MAGIC IS ALREADY STARTING TO WANE.

AND, AS THE CLOCK
FINALLY STRIKES TWELVE...
BONG

THE MAGIC RUNS OUT.
THE COACH TRANSFORMS BACK INTO A PUMPKIN.

THE HORSES TRANSFORM...

...BACK INTO MICE.

WAIT-WAIT, STOP!

OH.

ALL IS AGAIN AS IT WAS.

OH!

BUT THE CASTLE RIDERS ARE STILL AFTER THEM!

CINDERELLA AND HER FRIENDS JUST HAVE ENOUGH TIME TO GET OUT OF THE ROAD...

...BEFORE THE RIDERS
MAKE THEIR WAY PAST.

AS THEY PASS, THEY CRUSH THE
PUMPKIN THAT HAD BEEN A COACH.

...SCATTERING THE LAST
REMAINS OF MAGIC.

I'M SORRY.
I GUESS I FORGOT ABOUT EVERYTHING...
...EVEN THE TIME.
BUT IT WAS SO WONDERFUL.

AND HE WAS SO HANDSOME. AND WHEN WE DANCED...
OH, I'M SURE THAT EVEN THE PRINCE HIMSELF COULDN'T HAVE BEEN MORE...
...MORE... SIGH.

WELL, IT'S OVER, AND --
CINDERELLY, LOOK! LOOK!

YOUR SLIPPER!

DUH, YOUR SLIPPER, CINDERELLY!

OH!

THANK YOU.

THANK YOU SO MUCH... FOR EVERYTHING.

MEANWHILE, BACK AT THE CASTLE...
YOUR MAJESTY? I SEE NO POINT IN BEATING ABOUT THE BUSH.
I REGRET TO INFORM YOU, SIRE...
...THAT THE YOUNG LADY HAS DISAPPEARED.
LEAVING BEHIND ONLY THIS GLASS SLIPPER.

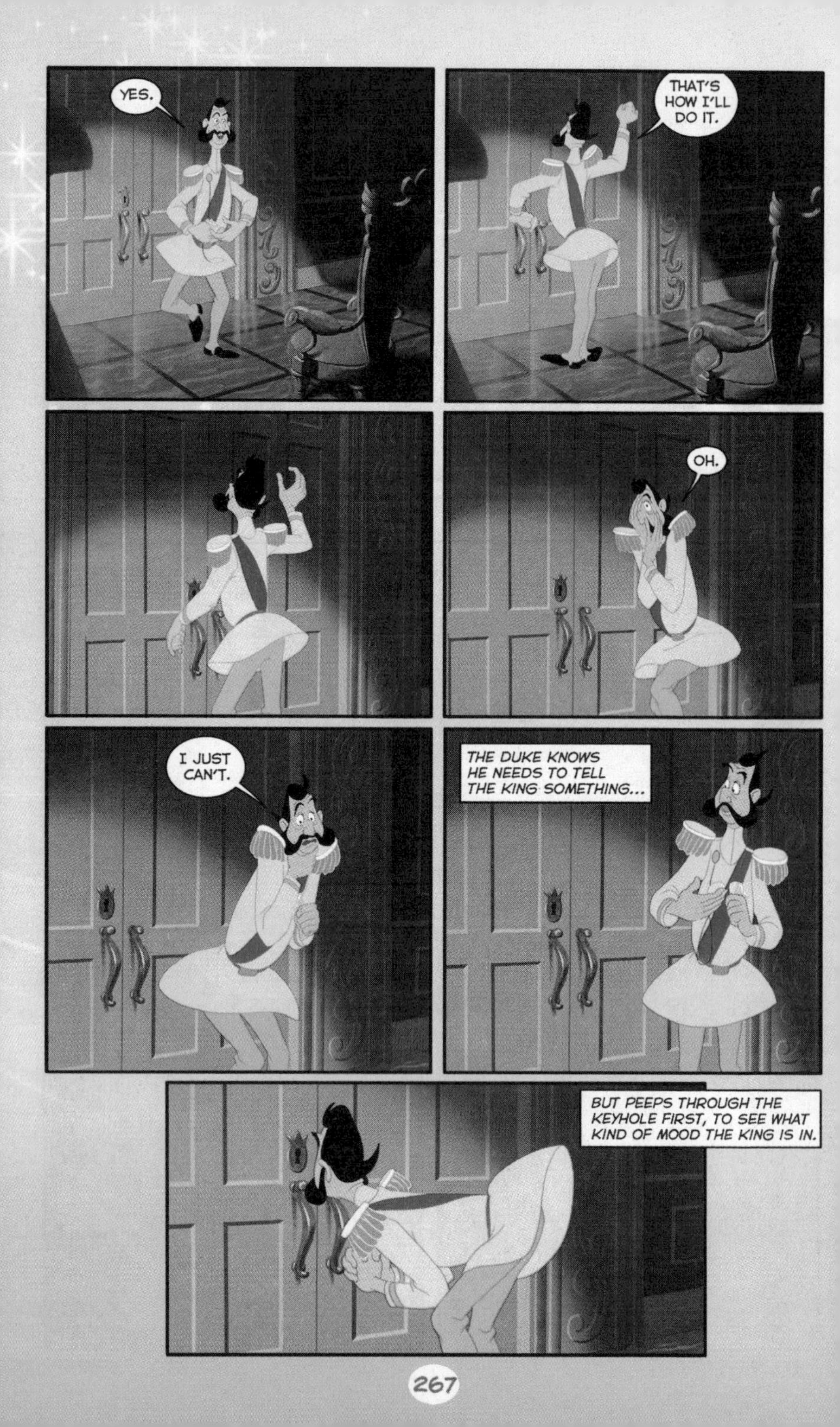
YES.
THAT'S HOW I'LL DO IT.
OH.
I JUST CAN'T.
THE DUKE KNOWS HE NEEDS TO TELL THE KING SOMETHING...
BUT PEEPS THROUGH THE KEYHOLE FIRST, TO SEE WHAT KIND OF MOOD THE KING IS IN.

ZZZZZZ
ZZZZZ
SSNXXXX-
ZZZZZ -
HA HA?
ZZZ-
HA HA HA HA
HO HO...
AHHH...

LAUGHTER MEANS A GOOD DREAM.
BUT WHAT DOES A KING DREAM ABOUT?
HA HA!
WHEE!

HA HA!
EH?
KNOCK
KNOCK
KNOCK

EH?

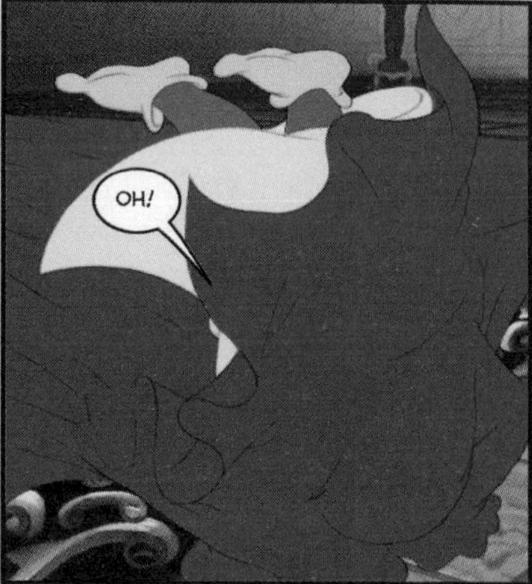
OH!

GRUMBLE

KNOCK
KNOCK
KNOCK

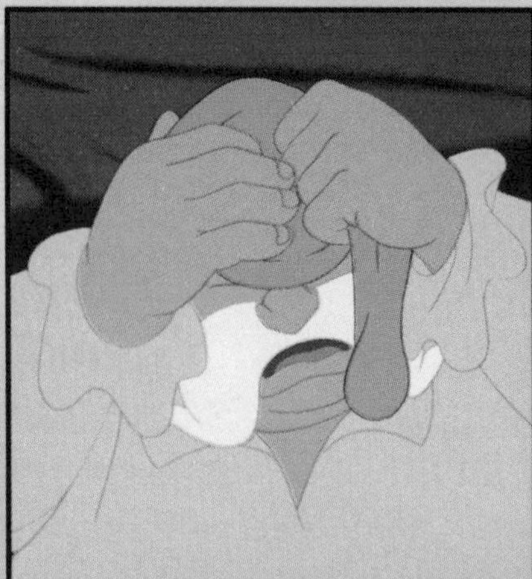

WELL?
COME IN!

COME IN!!!
YOUR MAJESTY --
SO!!!
HE'S PROPOSED ALREADY!
TELL ME ALL ABOUT IT!
WELL, SIRE --
WHO IS SHE?

WHERE DOES SHE LIVE?

AH--

WELL, I DIDN'T GET A CHANCE --

NO MATTER, WE'VE MORE IMPORTANT THINGS TO DISCUSS.

ARRANGEMENTS FOR THE WEDDING, INVITATIONS, A NATIONAL HOLIDAY...

ALL THAT SORT OF THING.
BUT, BUT SIRE!

HERE, HAVE A CIGAR!
TAKE A FEW MORE!
BETTER PRACTICE PASSING THESE OUT, EH?
BUT IF YOU'D ONLY LISTEN!
HA-HAH!
AND FOR YOU, MY FRIEND?
OH!

YOUR-YOUR MAJESTY, P-PLEASE!
A KNIGHTHOOD!
I HEREBY DUB YOU SIR...
ER...BY THE WAY, WHAT TITLE WOULD YOU LIKE?
SIRE? SHE GOT AWAY.
SHE GOT AWAY?

A PECULIAR TITLE, BUT IF THAT'S WHAT YOU -- WAIT.
SHE WHAT?
YOU... YOU... YOU TRAITOR!!
NO, SIRE! REMEMBER!
YOUR -- YOUR BLOOD PRESSURE!
TREASON!
SLICE

NO, SIRE! NO!
SABOTAGE!
YOU WERE IN LEAGUE WITH THE PRINCE ALL ALONG!
I TRIED TO STOP HER, BUT SHE VANISHED INTO THIN AIR!
A LIKELY STORY!
BUT IT'S TRUE, SIRE!
ALL WE COULD FIND WAS THIS GLASS SLIPPER!

THE WHOLE THING WAS A PLOT!
BUT SIRE, HE LOVES HER!

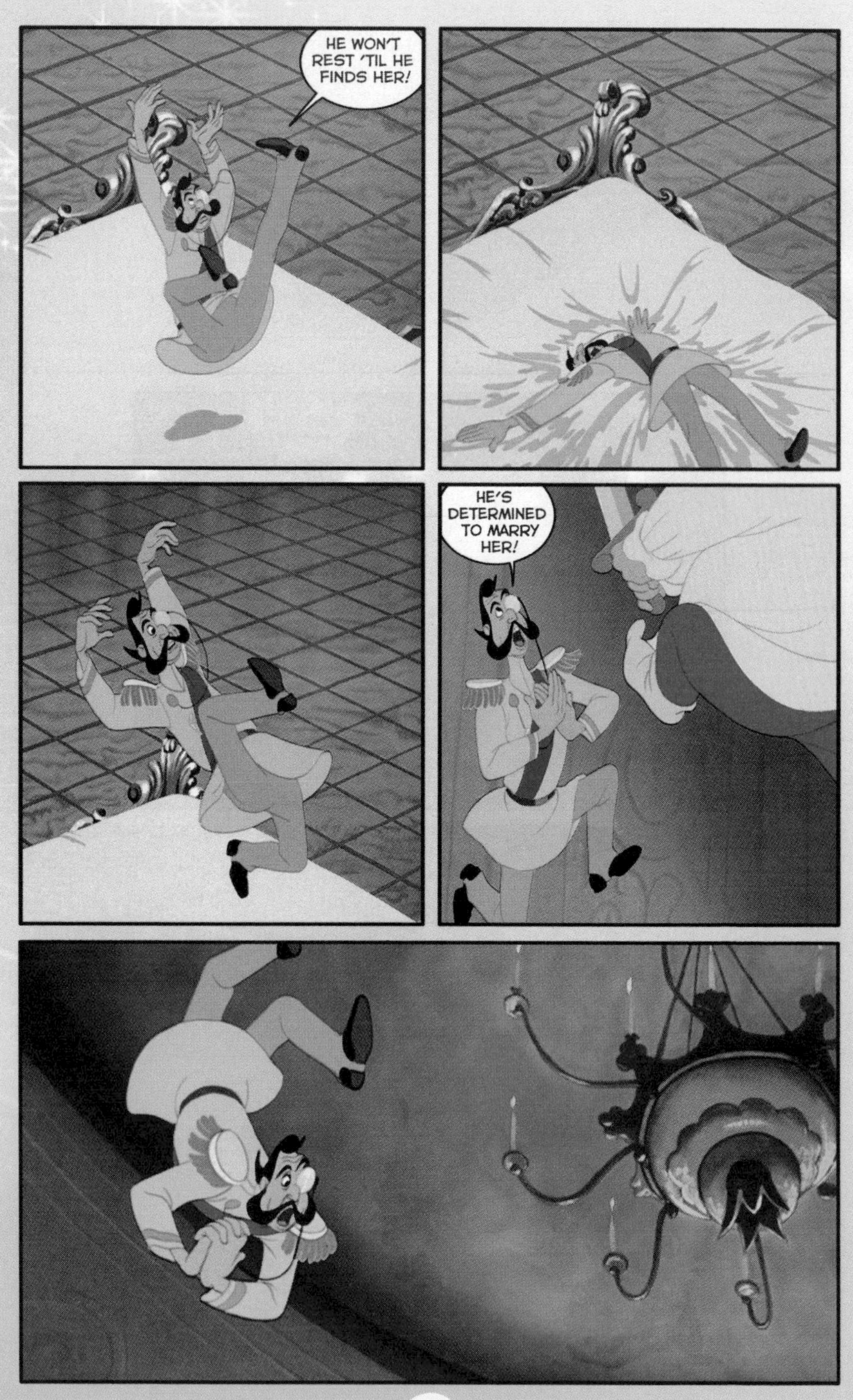
HE WON'T REST 'TIL HE FINDS HER!
HE'S DETERMINED TO MARRY HER!

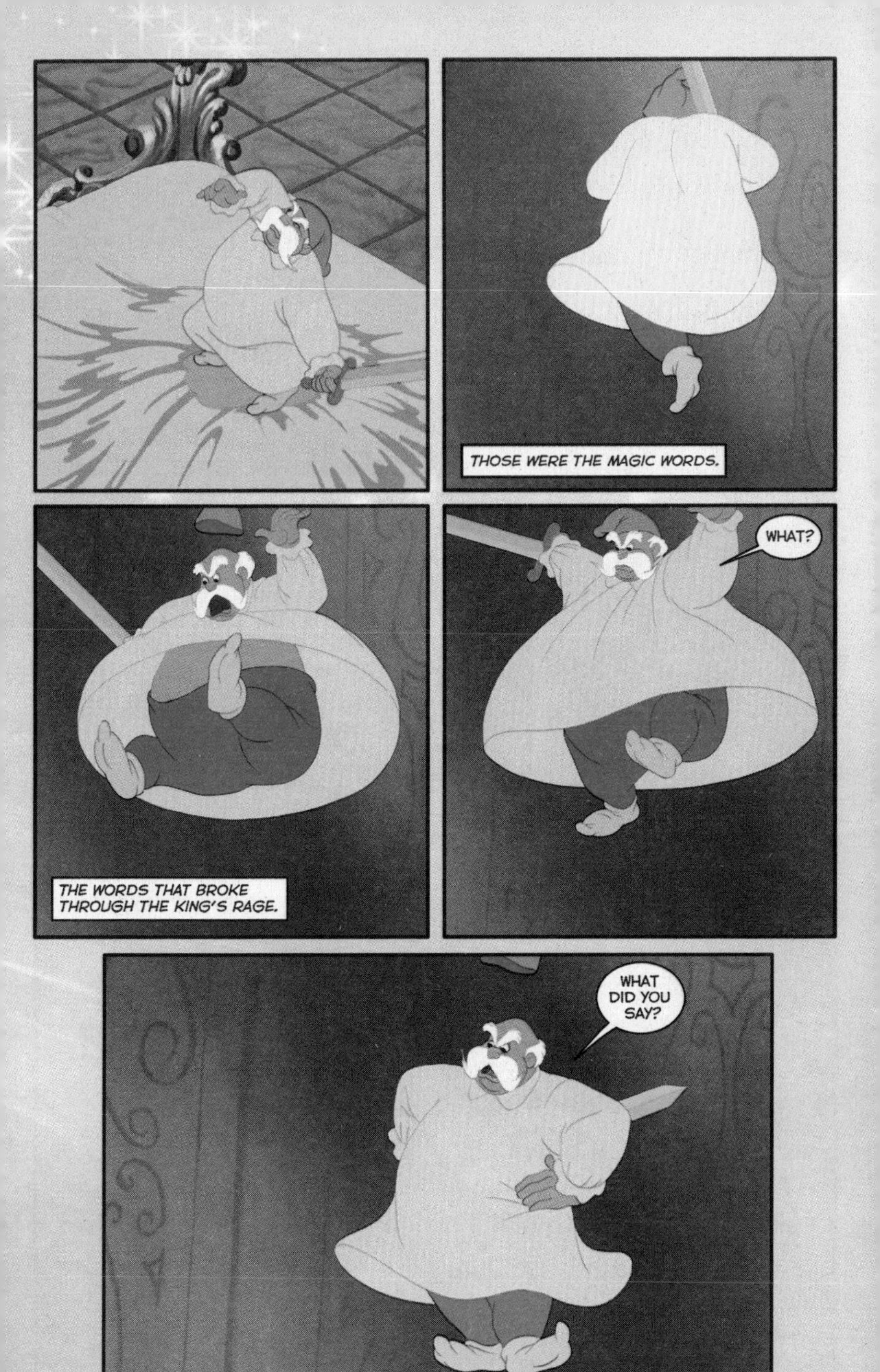
THOSE WERE THE MAGIC WORDS.
THE WORDS THAT BROKE THROUGH THE KING'S RAGE.
WHAT?
WHAT DID YOU SAY?

THE PRINCE, SIRE!
HE SWEARS THAT HE'LL MARRY NONE BUT THE GIRL WHO FITS THIS SLIPPER!
HE SAID THAT, DID HE?

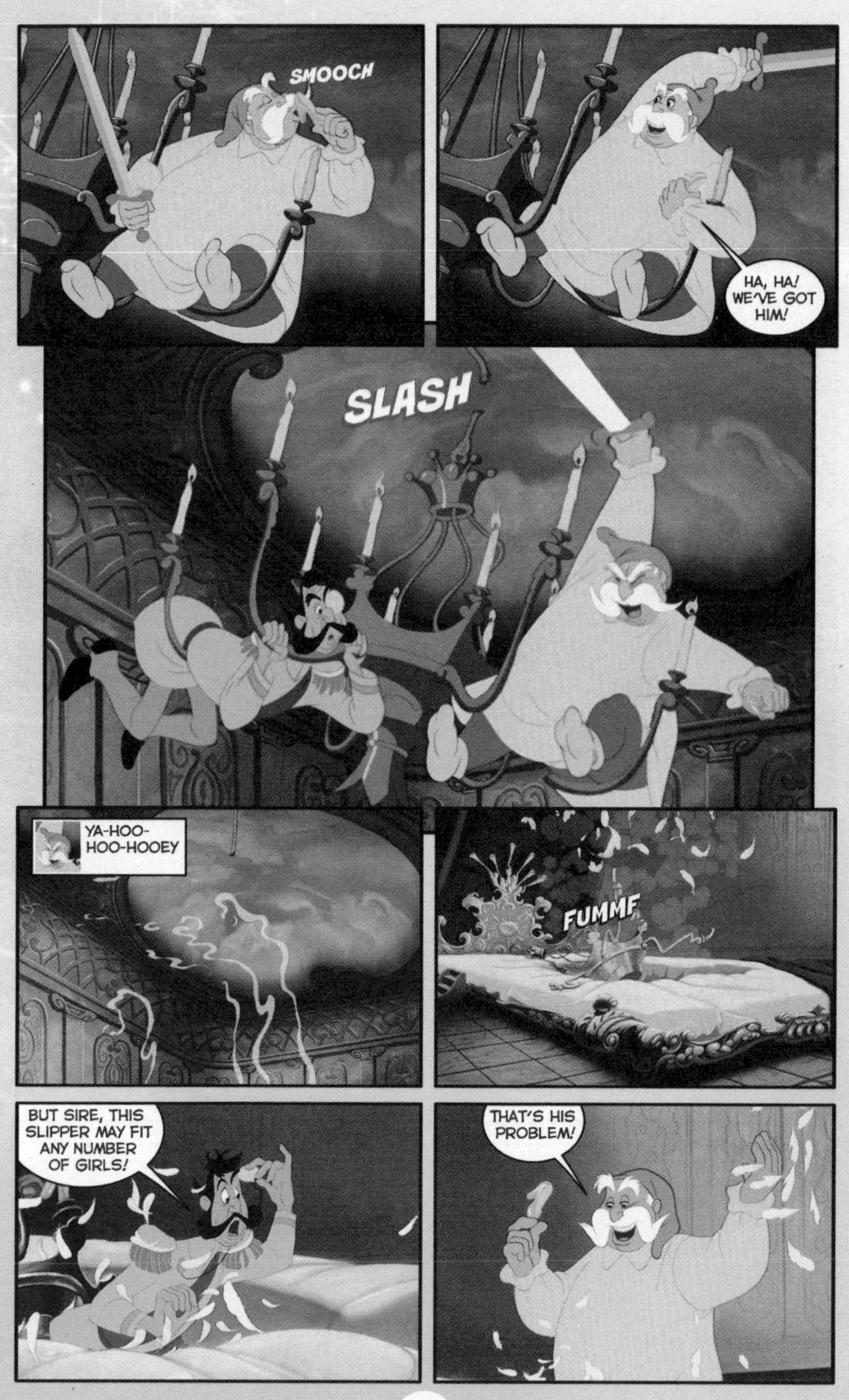
SMOOCH
HA, HA! WE'VE GOT HIM!
SLASH
YA-HOO-HOO-HOOEY
FUMMF
BUT SIRE, THIS SLIPPER MAY FIT ANY NUMBER OF GIRLS!
THAT'S HIS PROBLEM!

HE'S GIVEN HIS WORD, WE'LL HOLD HIM TO IT!
NO, YOUR HIGHNESS.
I'LL HAVE NOTHING TO DO WITH IT!
YOU'LL TRY THIS ON EVERY MAID IN MY KINGDOM!

AND IF THE SHOE FITS--

--BRING HER IN.

--I--

Y-YES, YOUR MAJESTY.

AND SO, THE NEXT MORNING, A PROCLAMATION WAS POSTED FOR ALL TO SEE...
By the King
A Proclamation
...ALERTING THE KINGDOM THAT EVERY MAIDEN SHOULD BE PREPARED TO TRY ON THE LEFT-BEHIND GLASS SLIPPER, BY ORDER OF THE KING.
CINDERELLA? CINDERELLA?
CINDERELLA!
OH, WHERE IS THAT GIRL?

YES? HERE I AM.
MY DAUGHTERS. WHERE ARE THEY?
I THINK THEY'RE STILL IN BED.
OHHH!
WELL, DON'T JUST STAND THERE! BRING UP THE BREAKFAST TRAYS AT ONCE -
AND HURRY!
WONDER WHATSA MATTER?
WHATSA MATTER WITH HER?
I DUNNO! LET'S FIND OUT! C'MON!

DRIZELLA. DRIZELLA!
YAWN
WHAT?
GET UP.
GET UP THIS INSTANT!
WE HAVEN'T A MOMENT TO LOSE!

ANASTASIA?
ANASTASIA!
GET UP, ANASTASIA!
WHAT FOR? WHY?
EVERYONE'S TALKING ABOUT IT, THE WHOLE KINGDOM!
OH, HURRY NOW - HE'LL BE HERE ANY MINUTE!

YAWN -- WHO WILL?
THE GRAND DUKE! HE'S BEEN HUNTING ALL NIGHT
HUNTING?
FOR THAT GIRL!
THE ONE WHO LOST HER SLIPPER AT THE BALL LAST NIGHT -
-- THEY SAY HE'S MADLY IN LOVE WITH HER!

THE DUKE IS?
NO, NO, NO -THE PRINCE!
GASP! THE PRINCE!
CRASH
WHAT --

YOU CLUMSY LITTLE FOOL!
CLEAN THAT UP, AND THEN HELP MY DAUGHTERS DRESS.
WHAT FOR?
IF HE' IN LOVE WITH THAT GIRL --
--WHY SHOULD WE EVEN BOTHER?
NOW YOU TWO LISTEN TO ME!
THERE IS STILL A CHANCE THAT ONE OF YOU CAN GET HIM.

ONE OF US?
WHY MOTHER, WHAT DO YOU MEAN?
JUST THIS: NO ONE, NOT EVEN THE PRINCE, KNOWS WHO THAT GIRL IS.
WE KNOW! WE KNOW!
SHHH!
THE GLASS SLIPPER IS THEIR ONLY CLUE!
THE DUKE HAS BEEN ORDERED TO TRY IT ON EVERY GIRL IN THE KINGDOM.

AND IF ONE CAN BE FOUND WHOM THE SLIPPER FITS, THEN, BY THE KING'S COMMAND...
THAT GIRL SHALL BE THE PRINCE'S BRIDE!
HIS BRIDE...
HIS BRIDE!!
CINDERELLA? GET MY THINGS TOGETHER!
NEVER MIND HER! MEND THESE RIGHT AWAY!
AS SOON AS SHE IRONS THESE!
MEND THIS!

WHAT'S THE MATTER WITH HER?
WAKE UP, STUPID!
WE'VE GOTTA GET DRESSED!
DRESSED.
OH, YES.
OH WE MUST GET DRESSED. IT WOULD NEVER DO FOR THE DUKETO SEE ME LIKE THIS...

DID YOU SEE WHAT SHE DID?
ARE YOU GOING TO JUST LET HER WALK AWAY?
QUIET.
AS CINDERELLA WALKS AWAY, SINGING TO HERSELF...
THE LADY TREMAINE FIGURES IT OUT.
CINDERELLA WAS THE MYSTERY GIRL.

WHAT'S SHE GONNA DO?
I DUNNO! GOTTA WATCH HER! C'MON!
QUIETLY THE LADY TREMAINE FOLLOWS CINDERELLA UP THE STAIRS...
AND THE MICE KEEP AN EYE ON HER.

JAQ AND GUS, BEING MUCH FASTER, REACH THE ATTIC BEFORE LADY TREMAINE.
THEY WATCH HER CLIMB THE STAIRS AND WONDER WHAT SHE COULD BE UP TO...
BEFORE DECIDING IT'D BE BEST NOT TO WAIT TO FIND OUT. THEY HAD TO WARN CINDERELLA!
CINDERELLY! CINDERELLY!
CINDERELLY! LOOK OUT!
BEHIND YOU!
OH NO!

LADY TREMAINE SAYS NOTHING; SHE JUST LOCKS THE ATTIC DOOR, AND REMOVES THE KEY...
...TRAPPING CINDERELLA.
OH YOU CAN'T DO THIS, YOU JUST CAN'T!
LET ME OUT! YOU MUST LET ME OUT!
YOU CAN'T KEEP ME IN HERE!
BUT THAT IS PRECISELY WHAT LADY TREMAINE INTENDS TO DO.

NO! NO, SHE CAN'T DO IT!
SHE CAN'T LOCK UP CINDERELLY! I'M GONNA--
SHH!
WE GOTTA GET THAT KEY, GUS-GUS! WE JUST GOTTA GET THAT KEY!

MEANWHILE...
ZZZZ...
HE'S A HERE! HE'S A HERE! A DUKE-DUKE!
A WHO?
A GRAND DUKE! WITH THE SLIPPER!
GOTTA GET THAT KEY!

OH, MOTHER! HE'S HERE! HE'S HERE!
THE GRAND DUKE!
DO I LOOK ALL RIGHT?
LET ME SEE THAT POWDER!
GIRLS, NOW REMEMBER -- THIS IS YOUR LAST CHANCE.
DON'T FAIL ME.

TA-ROO TA-ROO
ANNOUNCING HIS IMPERIAL GRACE, THE GRAND DUKE.
YOU HONOR OUR HUMBLE HOME.
AHEM. QUITE SO.

MAY I PRESENT MY DAUGHTERS --
DRIZELLA AND ANASTASIA
YOUR GRACE.
SHUDDER
AH, CHARMED, I'M SURE.
HIS GRACE WILL READ A ROYAL PROCLAMATION!
ALL LOYAL SUBJECTS OF HIS IMPERIAL MAJESTY ARE HEREBY... *YAWN*
...NOTIFIED BY ROYAL PROCLAMATION IN REGARDS TO A CERTAIN?
YAWN GLASS... SLIPPER.

IT IS UPON THIS DAY DECREED--
WHY, THAT'S MY SLIPPER!
WELL, I LIKE THAT. IT'S MY SLIPPER!
NO! CINDERELLY'S SLIPPER!
SHHH!

GIRLS, GIRLS!
YOUR MANNERS.
A THOUSAND PARDONS, YOUR GRACE. PLEASE CONTINUE.
YES. QUITE SO. UH... AH, YES.
IT IS UPON THIS DAY DECREED THAT A QUEST BE INSTITUTED ACROSS THE LENGTH AND BREADTH OF THIS DOMAIN...
THE SOLE AND EXPRESS PURPOSE OF THIS QUEST TO BE AS FOLLOWS --

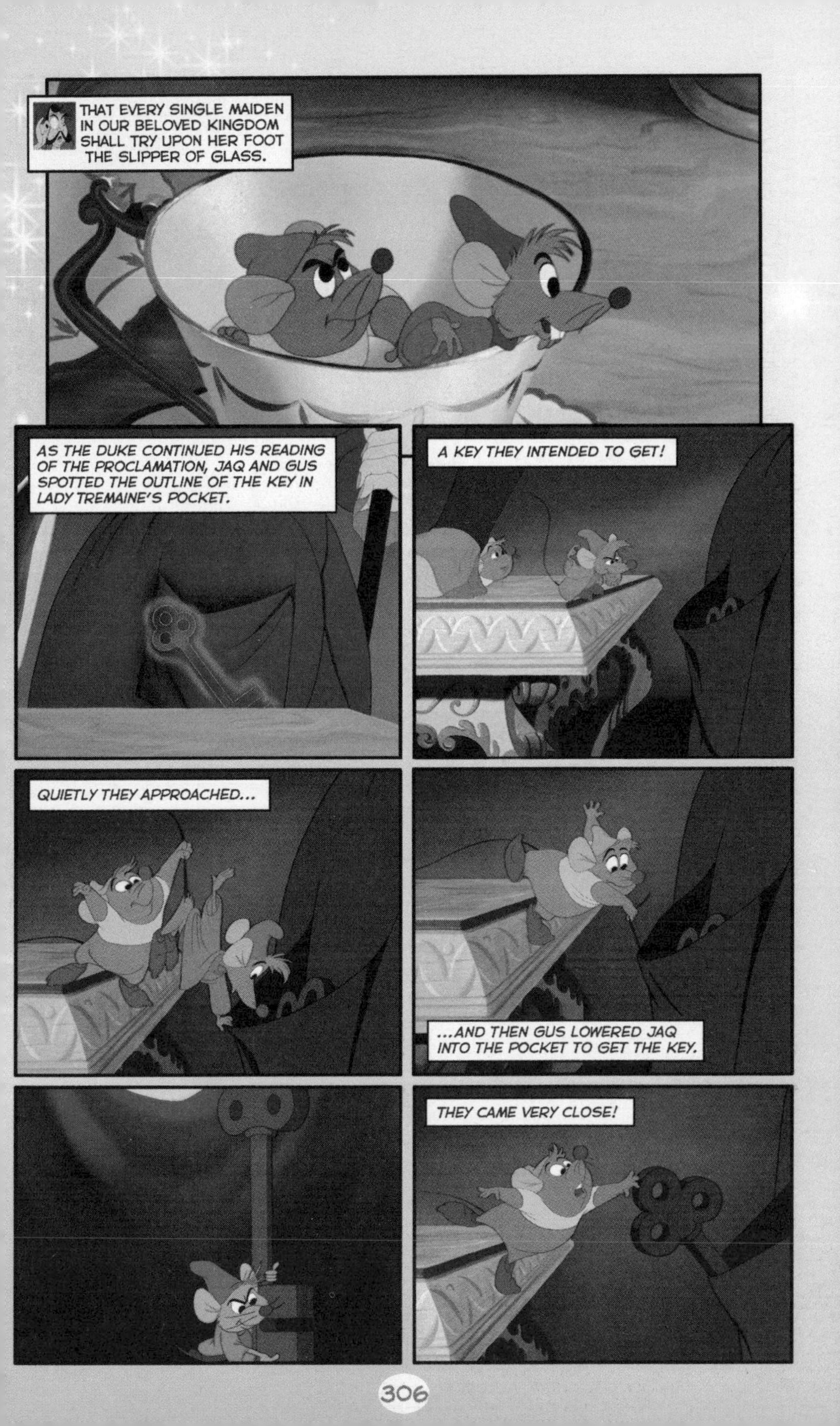
THAT EVERY SINGLE MAIDEN IN OUR BELOVED KINGDOM SHALL TRY UPON HER FOOT THE SLIPPER OF GLASS.
AS THE DUKE CONTINUED HIS READING OF THE PROCLAMATION, JAQ AND GUS SPOTTED THE OUTLINE OF THE KEY IN LADY TREMAINE'S POCKET.
A KEY THEY INTENDED TO GET!
QUIETLY THEY APPROACHED...
...AND THEN GUS LOWERED JAQ INTO THE POCKET TO GET THE KEY.
THEY CAME VERY CLOSE!

BUT THEN, LADY TREMAINE LOOKED TOWARD THE ATTIC, AND SCOWLED, THINKING OF HOW CINDERELLA HAD ALMOST RUINED THIS MOMENT.
GUS SAW HER REACHING TOWARDS THE KEY... PERHAPS TO MAKE SURE IT WAS STILL THERE.
JAQ PULLED THE KEY BACK INTO THE DRESS POCKET JUST IN TIME.
SATISFIED THE KEY WAS STILL THERE, LADY TREMAINE PATTED HER POCKET AND RETURNED HER ATTENTION TO THE GRAND DUKE.

...JUST IN TIME FOR HIM TO FINISH READING THE PROCLAMATION.
YAWN
SO BE IT.
YOU MUST BE QUITE FATIGUED, YOUR GRACE.
MAY WE OFFER YOU SOME TEA?
THANK YOU, MADAM, NO. WE MUST PROCEED WITH THE FITTING.
OF COURSE.

ANASTASIA, DEAR.
THERE! I KNEW IT WAS MY SLIPPER.
EXACTLY MY SIZE! I ALWAYS WEAR THE SAME SIZE.
AS SOON AS I SAW IT, I SAID --
OH!
WELL IT MAY BE A TRIFLE SNUG TODAY...

YOU KNOW HOW IT IS, DANCING ALL NIGHT...
I CAN'T UNDERSTAND WHY -- IT'S ALWAYS FIT PERFECTLY BEFORE!
I DON'T THINK YOU'RE HALF TRYING!
MOTHER, CAN YOU --
SHH. QUIET, MY DEAR.
WE MUSTN'T DISTURB HIS GRACE.
ZZZZZ...

YOUNG MAN, ARE YOU SURE YOU'RE TRYING IT ON THE RIGHT FOOT?
IT MUST HAVE SHRUNK OR SOMETHING. A GLASS SHOE ISN'T ALWAYS RELIABLE...
C'MON, GUS-GUS. WE GOT THE KEY, WE GOTTA GET IT UP THE STAIRS!
IF GETTING THE KEY HAD BEEN DIFFICULT...

BUT FOR CINDERELLA, THEY WOULD DO IT.
C'ON, GUS-GUS!
WHY CAN'T YOU HOLD STILL A MINUTE?
ENOUGH OF THIS!
THE NEXT YOUNG LADY, PLEASE.

HEAR THAT, GUS? HEAR THAT?
GOTTA HURRY!
DUH - YUP, HURRY!
C'MON! HURRY!
UH...

OHHH!
C'MON, GUS-GUS. JUST UP THERE.
C'MON!
IN HER ROOM, CINDERELLA IS QUIETLY SOBBING...
SO QUIETLY, SHE THINKS SHE HEARS SOMETHING ON THE OTHER SIDE OF THE DOOR!

US A'COMIN', CINDERELLY!
US'LL GET YOU OUT!
YOU'VE GOT THE KEY!
OH, HOW DID YOU EVER MANAGE TO --
CLOP

LUCIFER!
PLEASE LET HIM GO!
HEH HEH!
LET HIM GO!
LET HIM GO, LUCIFEE!
LET HIM GO!

CHOMP
MRRROOOW!!!
IT HAD BEEN A GOOD TRY BY JAQ...
...BUT NOT GOOD ENOUGH.
LUCIFER WAS DETERMINED TO NOT LOSE GUS AGAIN.

THE MICE, HOWEVER, WERE JUST AS DETERMINED TO FREE CINDERELLA (AND GUS, TOO!)
THEY ATTACKED WITH FORKS!

HAH!
BUT LUCIFER SWATTED THEM AWAY.
THEY TRIED FIRE!
SNORT.

PHEW

PFFT
...BUT LUCIFER BLEW IT OUT.

THERE WAS NOTHING THE MICE COULD DO TO MAKE HIM SET GUS FREE.
HA HA HA!

KR-KRASH

SO THE BIRDS TOOK A TURN, ASSAULTING THE WICKED CAT WITH DISHES.

MRROW!

FOR A MOMENT, WITH LUCIFER DISTRACTED, GUS WAS ABLE TO GET FREE!
BUT ONLY FOR A MOMENT.
CLOMP
BRUNO.
YES, BRUNO!
QUICK, GET BRUNO!
TWEET!
TWEET!

THE BIRDS FLY AS FAST AS THEY CAN, AND FIND BRUNO SLEEPING IN THE YARD.

THEY TRY THEIR BEST TO WAKE HIM...

...BUT END UP NEEDING HELP!
WHINNNEY!

NOW THAT BRUNO WAS AWAKE, ALL THE BIRDS NEEDED TO DO WAS GET HIM TO FOLLOW--!

UNNF!
OF ALL THE STUPID LITTLE IDIOTS --
I'LL DO IT MYSELF! GET AWAY FROM ME!
I'LL MAKE IT FIT!
IT FITS?
IT FITS?

DRIZELLA HAS INDEED SQUEEZED HER FOOT INTO THE SLIPPER...
POP
BUT IT DOESN'T STAY THERE LONG.
OH!
THE SLIPPER SPRINGS RIGHT OFF HER FOOT!
GASP!

THE DUKE AND THE HERALD BOTH SCRAMBLE TO CATCH IT!

WHEW.

OH, YOUR GRACE. I'M DREADFULLY SORRY. IT SHAN'T HAPPEN AGAIN.
PRECISELY, MADAM.

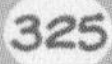

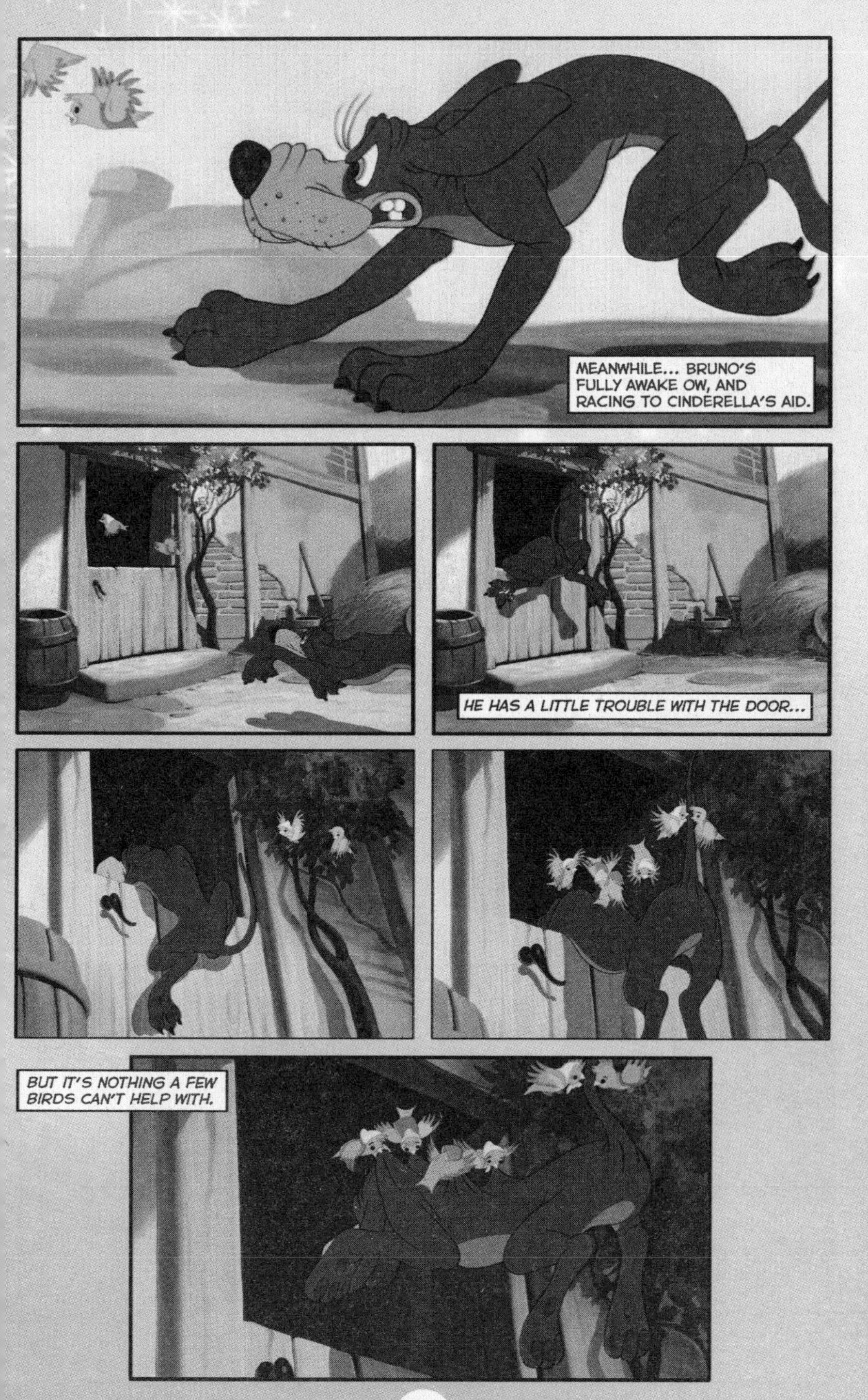
MEANWHILE... BRUNO'S FULLY AWAKE OW, AND RACING TO CINDERELLA'S AID.
HE HAS A LITTLE TROUBLE WITH THE DOOR...
BUT IT'S NOTHING A FEW BIRDS CAN'T HELP WITH.

PANT
PANT
WHEW
GRRR...
MRRROW!!
WOOF!

FSSST!
GRRR
WHUMP
LUCIFER IS AFRAID - HE KNOWS THERE'S NO ONE TO STOP BRUNO FROM TEARING HIM TO PIECES THIS TIME.
HE HAS TO ESCAPE, BUT THERE'S ONLY ONE EASY DIRECTION TO GO--
OUT THE WINDOW.
LUCIFER REALIZES THE FLAW IN THIS PLAN ON HIS LONG DROP TO THE GROUND.

C'MON!
GET UP!

GUS-GUS,
C'MON!
NOPE,
NOPE!
LET
GO!
GOTTA GET
THE KEY TO
CINDERELLY!

YOU ARE THE ONLY LADIES OF THE HOUSEHOLD, I HOPE --
ER, AH, I PRESUME?
THERE'S NO ONE ELSE, YOUR GRACE.
QUITE SO. GOOD DAY.
GOOD DAY--
YOUR GRACE!

YOUR GRACE!
PLEASE, WAIT! MAY I TRY IT ON?
OH, PAY NO ATTENTION TO HER.

IT'S ONLY CINDERELLA!
OUR SCULLERY MAID.
FROM THE KITCHEN!
IT'S RIDICULOUS! IMPOSSIBLE!

YES, JUST AN IMAGINATIVE CHILD!
MADAM --
--MY ORDERS WERE EVERY MAIDEN.
COME, MY CHILD.

THE DUKE SIGNALS FOR THE SLIPPER TO BE BROUGHT FORTH.

LADY TREMAINE KNOWS THAT THE SLIPPER WILL FIT, AND CINDERELLA WILL GET EVERYTHING SHE EVER WANTED.
SHE ALSO NOTICES THAT THE HERALD ISN'T WATCHING WHERE HE'S GOING...
AND STICKS OUT HER CANE EVER SO SLIGHTLY.
OOP!
GASP

KNASH
OH, NO!
NO, NO, NO--!
OH, THIS IS TERRIBLE!
THE KING!

WHAT WILL HE DO??
BUT PERHAPS, IF IT WOULD HELP --
NO, NO, NOTHING CAN HELP NOW.
NOTHING!

BUT YOU SEE --
I HAVE THE OTHER SLIPPER.

SMOOCH
HOORAY!
YEAH, CINDERELLY!
THE DUKE KNEELS DOWN TO PLACE THE SLIPPER ON CINDERELLA'S FOOT...
AND OF COURSE, IT FITS PERFECTLY.

NOT LONG AFTER THAT...
THE SOUND OF CHURCH BELLS RING THROUGHOUT THE KINGDOM...
...TO SIGNAL THE MARRIAGE OF CINDERELLA TO THE PRINCE.

THEY RACE DOWN THE PALACE STEPS TOGETHER.
AND WHEN CINDERELLA LOSES A SHOE THIS TIME --
SHE DOESN'T HAVE TO LEAVE IT BEHIND!

AND NO LESS THAN THE KING
HIMSELF KNEELS TO HELP HER.

KISS

BUT THE KING ISN'T
A RULER RIGHT NOW...

HE'S JUST A
HAPPY FATHER.

CINDERELLA'S
FRIENDS ARE
HAPPY TOO.
ESPECIALLY GUS --
WHO DISCOVERED THAT
RICE IS DELICIOUS.

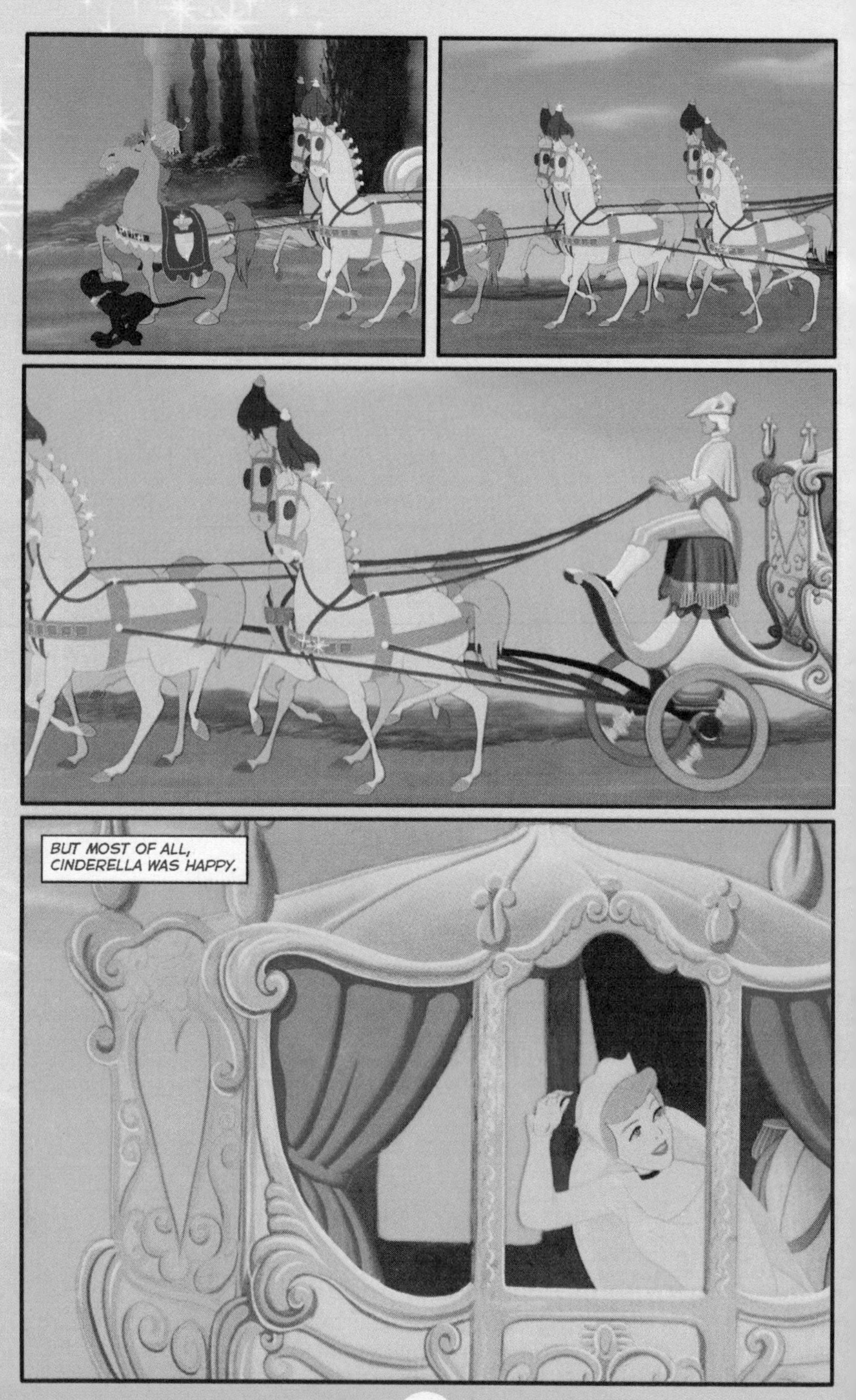
BUT MOST OF ALL,
CINDERELLA WAS HAPPY.

AND AS SHE RODE OFF WITH THE PRINCE, SHE REALIZED...
LOVE AND HAPPINESS. THIS WAS HER DREAM. THE WISH HER HEART HAD MADE.
AND IT HAD COME TRUE.

and they lived happily
ever after.
and they lived happily
ever after.
CINDERELLA
The End
A Walt Disney Production

With the Talents of

ILENE WOODS HELENE STANLEY
ELEANOR AUDLEY LUIS VAN ROOTEN
VERNA FELTON DON BARCLAY
CLAIRE DU BREY
RHODA WILLIAMS
JAMES MACDONALD

Special Processes UB IWERKS
Sound Director C. O. SLYFIELD
Sound Recording HAROLD J. STECK
ROBERT O. COOK
Film Editor DONALD HALLIDAY
Music Editor AL TEETER

APPROVED
MPAA
CERTIFICATE NO. 14033

COPYRIGHT MCMXLIX
WALT DISNEY PRODUCTIONS
ALL RIGHTS RESERVED

SOUND RCA SYSTEM

SCREEN CARTOONISTS

Musical Direction
OLIVER WALLACE
PAUL SMITH
Songs by
MACK DAVID JERRY LIVINGSTON
AL HOFFMAN
Orchestration JOSEPH DUBIN

Story
WILLIAM PEED ERDMAN PENNER
TED SEARS WINSTON HIBLER
HOMER BRIGHTMAN HARRY REEVES
KENNETH ANDERSON JOE RINALDI

Layouts

MAC STEWART A. KENDALL O'CONNOR

TOM CODRICK HUGH HENNESY

LANCE NOLLEY CHARLES PHILIPPI

DON GRIFFITH THOR PUTNAM

Color and Styling

MARY BLAIR JOHN HENCH

CLAUDE COATS DON DA GRADI

Backgrounds

BRICE MACK ART RILEY

RALPH HULETT RAY HUFFINE

DICK ANTHONY MERLE COX

THELMA WITMER

Directing Animators

ERIC LARSON WARD KIMBALL
MILT KAHL OLLIE JOHNSTON
FRANK THOMAS MARC DAVIS
JOHN LOUNSBERY LES CLARK
WOLFGANG REITHERMAN
NORM FERGUSON

Character Animators

DON LUSK PHIL DUNCAN
HUGH FRASER HAL KING
FRED MOORE HARVEY TOOMBS
JUDGE WHITAKER CLIFF NORDBERG
MARVIN WOODWARD HAL AMBRO
GEORGE NICHOLAS KEN O'BRIEN

Effects Animators

GEORGE ROWLEY JOSH MEADOR
JACK BOYD

Directors

WILFRED JACKSON

HAMILTON LUSKE

CLYDE GERONIMI

Production Supervision

BEN SHARPSTEEN

With the Additional Talents of

LUCILLE BLISS
MIKE DOUGLAS
MARION DARLINGTON
JOHN WOODBURY
JUNE FORAY
CLINT McCAULEY
HELEN SEIBERT

JOHN FONTAINE
WILLIAM PHIPPS
EARL KEEN
LUCILLE WILLIAMS
THURL RAVENSCROFT
JUNE SULLIVAN
BETTY LOU GERSON

Post Production Manager
DAVID CANDIFF

Post Production Coordinator
CORY HANSEN

Digital Color Timing Supervisor
BRUCE TAUSCHER

Animation Research Library

LELLA SMITH
TIM CAMPBELL
FOX CARNEY
DOUG ENGALLA
ANN HANSEN
TAMARA KHALAF
VIVIAN PROCOPIO
MATT TSUGAWA

THE LIBRARY OF CONGRESS
MOTION PICTURE CONSERVATION CENTER
DAYTON, OHIO

Nitrate Film Vault Leader GEORGE WILLEMAN

Nitrate Film Specialist IRWIN ROSENFELD

Motion Picture Restoration

LOWRY DIGITAL IMAGES, A DTS COMPANY

Project Manager JEFF SCHIFFMAN

Line Producer AMY BAILEY

Restoration Specialists

RACHEL J. CLEMENT
JIM CORBIN
DESTRY DORRO
ERIC FRANCISCO
ALFONSO GUERRERO JR.
NICHOLAS HERR
DYLAN HUCKLESBY
SEAN G. JAMIESON
BARRY KASS II
LOUISE KEATING
PAULA LAUTERBACH
KATRIN MOONEY
BRIDGID O'DONNELL
DANIEL ORTIZ
BRUCE PEECHER JR.
BENTON WONG

Digital Mastering by

TECHNICOLOR®
DIGITAL INTERMEDIATES
A TECHNICOLOR® COMPANY

Digital Colorist

TIMOTHY PEELER

Digital Producer

APRIL MCMORRIS

Re-recorded at

BUENA VISTA SOUND STUDIOS

Re-recording Mixers

KEITH ROGERS TERRY PORTER

Recordist

ERIK FLOCKOI

Sound Restoration by

ANDREAS K. MEYER

SONY MUSIC STUDIOS, NY

Special Thanks

S. J. BLEICK

KENT GORDON

MARY MEACHAM HOGG

CHRISTOPHER PINKSTON

HERMANN SCHMIDT

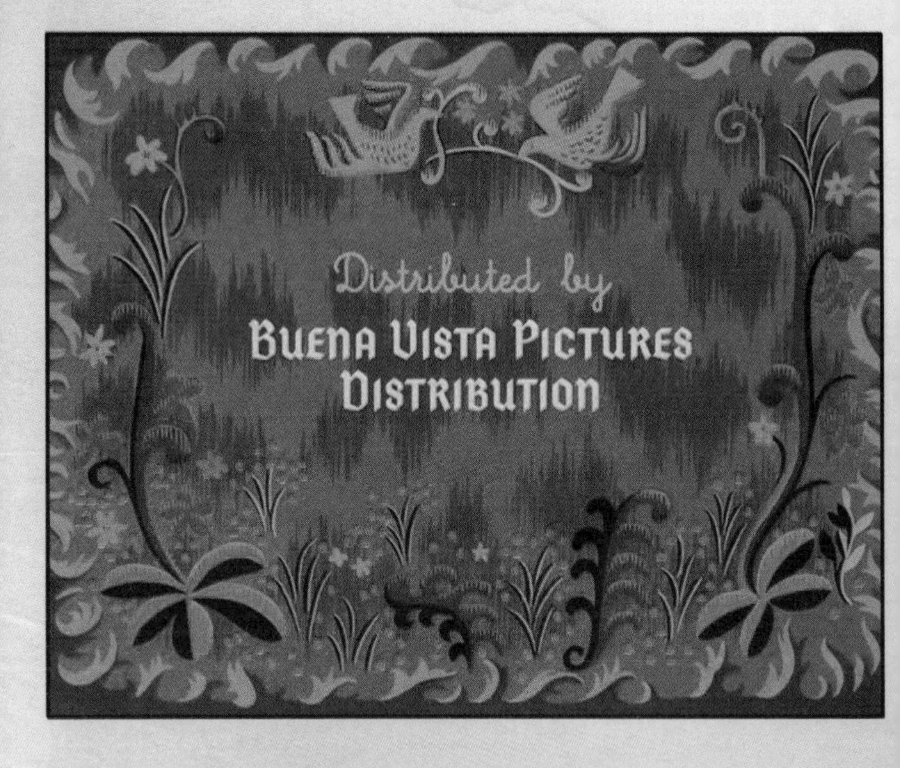
Distributed by
BUENA VISTA PICTURES
DISTRIBUTION

Walt Disney
presents
JOE BOOKS
CINESTORY
PREVIEW
One Hundred and One
Dalmatians
TECHNICOLOR®
Story
Bill Peet
Based on the book
"The Hundred And One Dalmatians" by... Dodie Smith

"MY STORY BEGINS IN LONDON, NOT SO VERY LONG AGO.
"YET SO MUCH HAS HAPPENED SINCE THEN, THAT IT SEEMS LIKE AN ETERNITY.
"AT THAT TIME I LIVED WITH MY PET IN A BACHELOR FLAT JUST OFF REGENTS PARK.
"IT WAS A BEAUTIFUL SPRING DAY, A TEDIOUS TIME OF THE YEAR FOR BACHELORS.
"OH... THAT'S MY PET, ROGER. ROGER RADCLIFF, A MUSICIAN OF SORTS. HA-HA. NO, NO..."

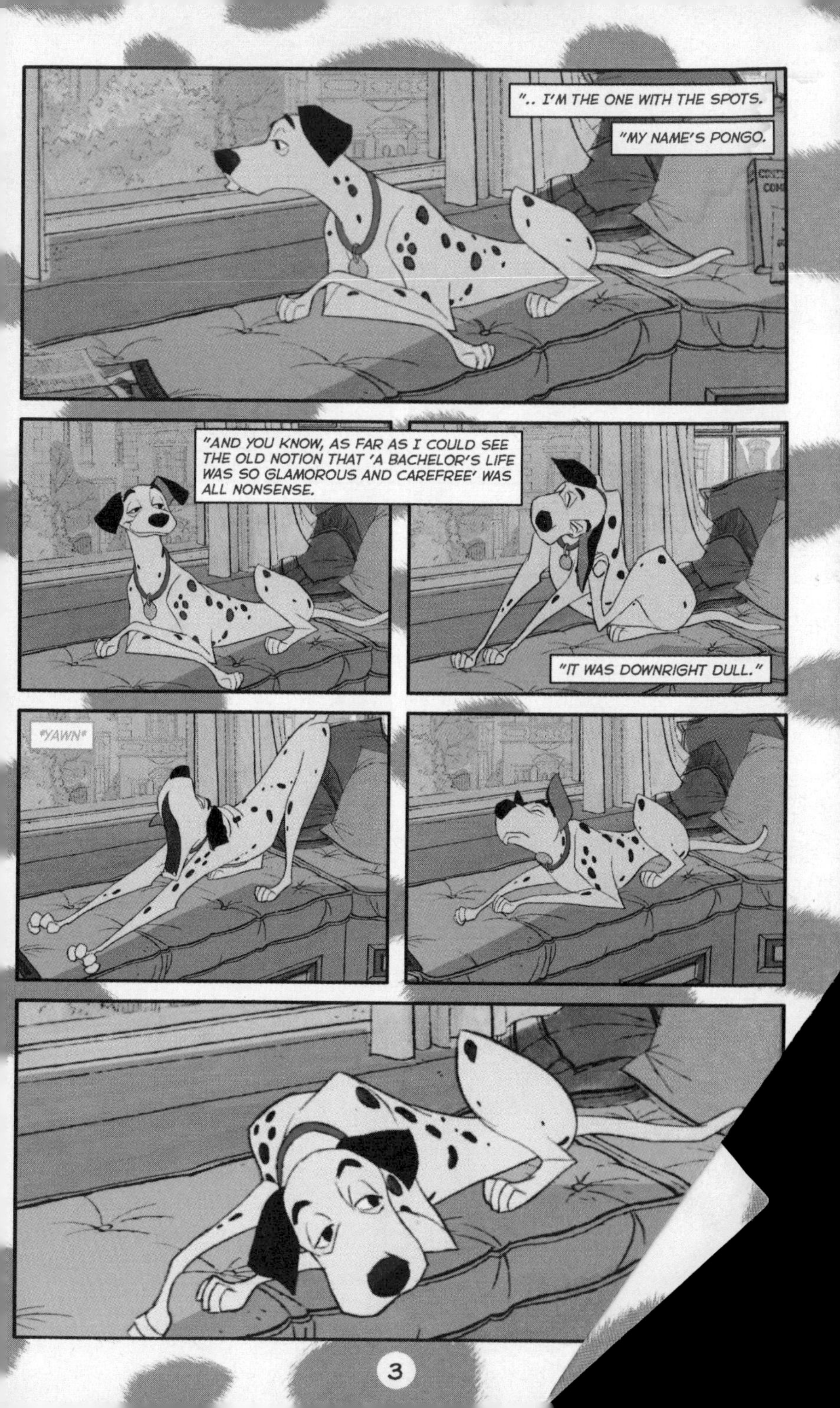
".. I'M THE ONE WITH THE SPOTS.
"MY NAME'S PONGO.
"AND YOU KNOW, AS FAR AS I COULD SEE THE OLD NOTION THAT 'A BACHELOR'S LIFE WAS SO GLAMOROUS AND CAREFREE' WAS ALL NONSENSE.
"IT WAS DOWNRIGHT DULL."
YAWN

"IT WAS PLAIN TO SEE THAT MY
OLD PET NEEDED SOMEONE.
"IF IT WERE LEFT UP TO ROGER,
WE'D BE BACHELORS FOREVER.
"HE WAS MARRIED TO HIS
WORK, WRITING SONGS.
"SONGS ABOUT ROMANCE... OF
ALL THINGS, SOMETHING HE KNEW
ABSOLUTELY NOTHING ABOUT.
"OH, HE'S INTELLIGENT
ENOUGH AS HUMANS GO.
"AND I THINK YOU COULD SAY, ROGER
IS A RATHER HANDSOME ANIMAL IN HIS WAY."

"I COULD SEE NO REASON WHY MY PET DIDN'T DESERVE AN ATTRACTIVE MATE...
"...BUT AT LEAST I WAS DETERMINED TO DO MY BEST.
OF CHIVALRY
"OF COURSE, DOGS ARE A PRETTY POOR JUDGE OF HUMAN BEAUTY..."
THE AGE OF CHIVALRY
A NEW COMPLETE STORY BY PERKINS

TWO SHILLIN
ST-SEPTEMBER
"...BUT I HAD A ROUGH IDEA OF WHAT TO LOOK FOR."
BREED."

"VERY UNUSUAL.
"HMM!
"OH, SURELY NOT.
"WELL NOW, WHAT HAVE WE HERE?
"HMM. WELL, A LITTLE...
"...TOO SHORT COUPLED."

"NOPE! I SAY!
"WELL, I DO SAY!
"NOW THERE'S A FANCY BREED.
"HMM.
"PERHAPS A LITTLE TOO FANCY.
"YES, MUCH TOO FANCY."

"OH! TOO OLD.
"TOO YOUNG.
"IT WAS A PROBLEM, A REAL PROBLEM.
"WELL, NOW --
"-- THAT'S A BIT MORE LIKE IT!"

"THE MOST BEAUTIFUL CREATURE ON FOUR LEGS! NOW IF ONLY THE GIRL...
"WELL!
"SHE'S VERY LOVELY TOO!
"IT WAS ALMOST TOO GOOD TO BE TRUE. "
READ THE REST IN STORES NOW!